BROKEN

HEARTS

BROKEN HEARTS

SEHDEV BISMAL

ISBN: 978-1-7923-0869-7

Cover design & interior formatting:
Mark Thomas / Coverness.com

Dedicated to the unflinching support of Bhajan who has made this book possible.
She is the inspiration behind most of these stories.

I

———

Is it the same place where I was born and brought up in?

Questions, unending questions, swarming, jumbled, chaotic questions preyed on her mind. The place looked completely foreign to her – perhaps another town had usurped her parents' village and morphed into an expanding, inchoate place.

She asked the driver to stop and got out of the juddering asthmatic motor contraption universally known as a tempo in India.

She went into a store and asked the shopkeeper: "*Sat Sri Akaal.* Where is Kishan Singh's house?" The shopkeeper looked at her as if she had descended from another world.

Who? He had never heard of Kishan Singh, her father.

Kirti's son, Amul, was sitting in the tempo looking slightly bemused, but also visibly bored. After a couple of further enquiries, Kirti found herself standing in front of the row of shops. A grocery shop, a confectionery store with *jalebis* and *laddus* on display in trays with a jostling crowd of flies and bees gorging on them. There was another non-descript shop next to this in which the shopkeeper was lying on his side on a makeshift large cushion, snoring spasmodically, but loudly, and, even in his sleep, perfunctorily trying to hit the invading flies with his hand.

The bazaar was teeming with people, despite the searing heat pouring from the skies. Inside some of the shops, the air-conditioning kept everyone comfortably cool. A large number of people were there in those shops, seemingly browsing, but trying to save themselves from the scorching furnace outside.

Kirti stared at the shopping complex, but she couldn't figure out precisely where the family house used to be – the house in which she had left many bittersweet memories embalmed, hoping to resurrect them one day.

With a heavy heart, she returned to the tempo and asked the driver to take her back to the train station. She decided to go back to the comforts of the hotel in Ludhiana where she and her son were staying to continue mourning the loss of the house where so many of her fond memories were buried.

About seven years ago, she'd first lost her father and then Balwant, her mother. She had not been back to India to see them again once she had left for England all those years ago. Her brother, Saninder, had gone to Dubai through an agent in the village too. He was working there on a building site and life was harsh, the treatment by the contractors meted out on him and his fellow labourers was brutal, untouched by pity.

The house where they'd spent their childhood had collapsed some three years ago under the weight of torrential monsoons. The village council or *panchayat* had taken over the land underneath the rubble and sold it to a developer in order to build three shops. Kirti had wanted to have a last look at the place where dreams of freedom and a carefree life had once filled her mind with an irrepressible sense of joy.

She went back to Ludhiana and sank into a chair, feeling abandoned, utterly despondent, recalling the high points of her early days before life decided to break her reverie. She mourned the loss of her parents' house and the loss of her childhood.

The distressing loss of her childhood did not only happen on the day of her visit though. Something had begun to steal her innocence almost twenty years ago when she thought she was being ejected from her home to move to a foreign country.

How she wished for Maninder to be there to hear her cries and offer a few soothing words of consolation!

Finding herself in a strange place, another continent, Kirti could vividly recall the moments when she was like a butterfly with broken wings, frantically trying to fly out of her gilded cage.

Sinking deeper and deeper into an interminable winter, the murky, unkissed-by-sun English winter with everything around her in perennial damp, Kirti often asked herself: "Why? What I have I done to deserve this life, much of which is being spent chasing a mirage and not of my choosing either?" She remembered the frozen pavement in her street, the slushy roads, some of the shrubs and plants overwhelmed by the sheer weight of snow. She'd seen a few neighbours struggling to avoid a fall whenever they ventured out.

She constantly looked back at the life she had lived before landing in London.

It involved not having enough money and a very simple lifestyle, away from the latest fashion trends one encounters in big cities but, nevertheless, it was a life which assured security, unfettered affection from her family and the freedom to gaze at skies, clouds and stars and the verdant fields surrounding her village.

Where had it all gone? Picking mustard leaves on the family farm, drinking homemade *lassi* and eating freshly churned butter with a *paratha*, playing games with her best friends and being looked after by doting, undemanding parents – memories of what she had left behind often triggered a choking feeling in her oesophagus. The contrast with what she was currently experiencing in England was utterly debilitating. The realisation that she was dependent upon others who up until a few weeks ago were complete strangers to her, filled her mind with an unforgiving chill.

She had relished her freedom and choice when she was young – playing, studying, gossiping, frolicking. Though from a fairly large family with three brothers, she was the only girl-child and received special attention from her parents, probably because she was the youngest in the family, almost an afterthought. Her parents regarded her as a gift from God in the fast approaching twilight of their lives.

Her world changed irrevocably when she was despatched to England. She had heard so much about the country, how it was the land of milk and honey and how many immigrants from India there had amassed wealth through hard work. She did not realise that reality was a completely different beast. A false picture of fortune had been painted by many immigrants on their occasional return visits to India. Their ego or their desperate search for recognition from their relatives and community made them build imaginary edifices of fortune. Now that she was here, Kirti's fragile dreams were collapsing around her and there was nothing she could do to travel back to the past.

There, she was now reduced to simply waiting for Ranjit to come home, even when she knew it was going to be a futile wait, as ever, draining all colour from her dreams.

2

Kirti's nightmare had started some eighteen years ago.

She was in a small room, slightly dingy and murky. Close to the dark brown freckled ceiling, there was an opening which served as exit for smoke and the pungent, spicy smells of cooking. She often sat in that room which served as a kitchen, storeroom and pantry with her eyes fixed on the ceiling. She could see, on occasion, many patterns – parts of weird animals' anatomies and tracings by unseen ghostly hands. There was a single light bulb hanging naked from a cable, diffusing its watery light in a half-hearted way, without much success most of the time, but more so in the evenings. The walls had not seen a coat of paint for years, so a dark sheen spread-eagled in all directions. There was a fire reluctantly burning in the clay *chulha*, phlegmatic smoke billowing towards the ceiling. The haze hanging in the air reminded Kirti of the smog in Ludhiana that she had experienced while going to her secondary school there on December mornings.

Her mother had left a small aluminium saucepan on the hearth, with some yellow lentils simmering away gently and some chopped onions and tomatoes floating on the surface. Kirti noticed the saucepan was pockmarked with dozens of small dents and that its bottom was black with soot.

Kirti left her schoolbag of text and exercise books with some odd biros and pencils swilling around by the wall outside the kitchen door. She sat down on a makeshift stool in a shady corner to have a glass of water from an earthen pitcher. The drink was soothing after having walked a couple of miles from her school in the blazing sun. She mopped the sweat off her brow with the end of her light brown *chunni*.

The heat of the summer sun ferociously invaded the kitchen and there were logs burning in many a stove in the homes in Haripur, her village.

Kirti was deliberately trying to slow down the trickle of cool water cascading down her throat to prolong the comforting sensation. A couple of minutes later, her mother came in to stoke the recalcitrant hearth fire with a wooden stick.

Her mother sat and blew down a hollow bamboo pipe to coax the fire. She looked slightly bedraggled, strands of her white hair trying to flee away from their roots, her clothes looking forlorn, needing a wash and a change. Kirti felt sorry for her. Her mother, Balwant, had spent all her adult life bringing up four children while their resources had remained resolutely scarce.

She suddenly looked at Kirti and said: "Kirti, your father wants to have a word with you. Cover your head and listen to him with respect."

Kirti missed a heartbeat as this usually signalled something ominous. A small, but quite perceptible shiver ran down her spine. She knew that her father did not frequently have conversations with her. He was a man of few words, calm at times, relaxed, but he did not find it easy to talk to people. If he was happy, or burdened by any anxiety, his eyes would often communicate his feelings instead.

A couple of minutes later, her father, Kishan Singh, came into the kitchen, wiped the sweat off his face with the loose end of his once-white, but now a distinctly greyish turban and sat on a low stool with a seat of hemp strings. He looked even more dishevelled than her mother, his beard being almost white and unkempt. His turban, with a long loose end hanging over his shoulder, could have done with some coaxing and cajoling as well. His eyes looked tired, glazed with ennui. Kirti felt sorry for him. He'd been a good father, caring in a self-effacing way, leaving the frontline support to her mum. Surely, he needed someone to look after him, to occasionally spoil him and pick him up from the floor when crestfallen.

Kishan cleared his throat, took a sip of cold water from the earthen pitcher and without any preface, without even looking at her face, said, "Kirti, I have found the boy that you are going to marry. He lives in England. He has a good job there and works in a garage. I think he owns that garage, so I am told.

Your uncle Milkha Singh knows the family very well. The boy, his name is Ranjit, lives with his family, drives a motor car and has a good future. If you go over there, you will enjoy the comforts of life there. I have said yes and Ranjit will be coming to India to meet you and tell us if he is willing to marry you. So, pray to Waheguru, God, that he finds you acceptable and all right to be his wife. You will lead a life of luxury, *beti*, my daughter, and we can spend the rest of our life without having to worry about your future."

Perhaps to justify his decision to agree so readily to Ranjit's visit, he carried on. "Kirti, I know it must have come as a shock to you. But, *beti*, we cannot feel relaxed until you are married. Once you are settled in your new home, your mum and I plan to go on a pilgrimage to a few *gurdwara*. I know the blessings of Waheguru are with you. You are a good daughter and you will know that what we are doing is only for your future."

Kirti could not see any discernible signs of elation in his voice. He was doing his fatherly duty by trying to ensure a good future for his daughter, but there were no tiny explosions of anticipation or joy in his words. He avoided making any eye contact with Kirti while he was sharing this seismic news with her.

While her father was speaking, Kirti had her gaze fixed on the floor. She didn't know what to say or how to react. She knew that finding a suitable groom for her was going to be difficult, given the present state of the family's finances.

The very mention of a foreign country, nevertheless, stirred her blood and she felt she could dare to have some dreams of a better life there. Kirti remembered her friend Sharna's sister, Rani, who had gone over to England and said that life was much better there than in India. Whenever she returned to India to visit her parents, she would go the nearest town and purchase rolls and rolls of fabric to be made into *shalwar kameez* by the local tailor. All those who knew her used to watch her with mouths open in amazement, envious of her good fortune.

Kirti could feel a slight shaking within her body, shaking in anticipation of life in Villayat, England. She knew another girl, Sundeep, who was a couple of years senior to her at school, who had talked about her life in a foreign country during her visit to India a couple of years ago.

"Girls have lots of freedom there, they can buy their own things in big shops, they can go out on their own without an escort and their husbands buy them presents every Friday," she said, making many of her friends salivate and have reveries as they often did when watching suggestive, saccharine scenes in Bollywood movies.

The very thought of going abroad, having a married, settled life in a house of one's own – it all sounded the stuff of fairy tales. In her village, life was very regulated and most people, girls in particular, were conditioned not to have any dreams. They were rather rooted in the harsh realities of day-to-day life.

Kirti, like most of the girls in her village followed a strict regime of activities which did not change and left no room for creative planning. Almost all of her friends were content living in a similar milieu. When they had a chance to see or talk about Bollywood movies, they used to have fantasies and sometimes conversations about the freedoms the actors and their characters enjoyed. They would talk about the mouth-watering ways the actors could express their desires, yearnings or frustrations. They, on the other hand, were the mute denizens of their village society, having no say in the decisions affecting their lives. They sometimes talked about similar dreams, but only as a game. They knew they would never be allowed to realise those dreams in the real world. And, somehow, they didn't really miss those freedoms either because they had never experienced them.

Kirti did not respond to her father and kept her eyes fixed on the floor. Her silence signalled her acceptance of his behest and that would please him. He looked at his daughter and added in a relieved tone: "May Waheguru bless you, my child!"

That night Kirti couldn't get a wink of sleep. Living in a strange, unknown environment without the immediate supportive presence of her parents, coming to terms with the way of living in a different culture and then the deliciousness of having a physical relationship with a husband – Kirti's mind was in turmoil.

Richa, one of Kirti's best friends at school, had shown her several books in which boys and girls were free to choose their own partner. Some of the books were in English, but many had been translated into Punjabi. Kirti did not have many books at home, apart from her school books.

Although her father owned some agricultural land where

11

he grew wheat, maize and sometimes rice, the cost of buying fertilisers, hiring manual labour at planting and harvesting times and renting machinery for ploughing and sowing meant there was not much money left for luxuries, such as books, electrical gadgets or even occasional presents. Usually birthdays within the family were marked by cooking an extra dish and making a dessert, such as *halva* or *khir*, rice pudding, before the obligatory prayers were offered.

Richa's life seemed to be another life to Kirti, a Narnia version of what she herself was living. Richa's father was a shopkeeper selling fabrics and had a huge number of customers from the surrounding villages. Also, she was the only daughter in the family and her parents tried to give her a choice in clothes and presents on special occasions. Kirti would see her immersed in her books during her visits to her house and Richa would wistfully talk of the unfettered delights characters in those books enjoyed as a matter of routine.

Kirti, however, felt that she was not really missing anything. If she managed to make her parents happy through conforming or accepting their norms, then that would be sufficient to make her contented, she thought. But listening to her school friends and, on occasion, while watching Bollywood movies, she could see there was another world out there, away from her village and immediate family life. She would feel surprised at the awakening of strange dreams about her future where she could pursue her own happiness, rather than trying to please others.

It was Vaisakhi time and she was getting ready to go the

village *gurdwara* to say her prayers. Although they lived in a small village, there were already two *gurdwara* within touching distance of each other. The blaring of music from loudspeakers from each of them filled the air of every home and every room in the village before dawn. Her mum shouted from the kitchen where she spent most of her time cooking, preparing for cooking or cleaning utensils or blowing hard at the slumbering embers in the *chulha*.

"Kirti, try to come back from the *gurdwara* soon, Ranjit is coming to our house to see you. He will be travelling from Amritsar after landing and will come straight to our village. And make sure you have a good *salwar kameez* on and a good *chunni*."

Her heart leapt, not with joy, but with fear. What if Ranjit rejected her, what if he found her too simple, too rustic and unsophisticated? Even when she was offering prayers in the *gurdwara*, her mind was on his visit and her whole body experienced minor tremors of fright. If he accepted her that would be a huge relief, so she was trying to find something positive to calm her inner turbulence. After all, that would also make her mum and dad happy. Kirti felt slightly guilty though when several awkward questions plagued her mind: "What if I don't find Ranjit attractive enough? Is there anyone else who would seek my acceptance? What if he has body odour? Or a fiery temper?" She tried to brush aside similar bristling thoughts. But the idea of pleasing her parents forced her to restrain her imagination.

In most of the folk songs played on the loudspeakers in

her village at weddings, festivals and family days, the lyrics always gushed about feelings of love. What was this love? She often used to wonder as these songs of love accompanied by convoluted dancing featured in most Bollywood movies. Everywhere music professed love, but it usually also expressed the depth of despair due to unrequited affection or mourning widening distances between lovers.

She still remembered, with a shudder of delight she was ashamed to confess, the time when Sukhi had touched her arm and tried to hold her hand. Sukhi was her friend Baljit's' older brother, a couple of years senior to her. He had left the village to study at a college in the nearby town, Phagwara.

She had gone to her father's fields to pick some *saag* and mustard leaves, when suddenly he had appeared in front of her. She did not know how to respond or what to say. She was feeling red and hot, wondering what she should fix her eyes on when he'd touched her arm. The goose bumps on her arms felt massive, little rounded hills soon appearing all over her body. He said something about how much he would love to be her friend and then he held her hand with a slightly firm grip. A tsunami of fear had rushed through her heart, but, somehow, she found the experience rather exhilarating.

He was wearing a checked shirt and light brown trousers with a sharp crease. His clothes must be the latest fashion in the city, she thought. His light brown eyes were focused on her and his hand felt soft, supple and inviting. Was this the way to start a story of love?

Kirti had withdrawn her hand abruptly and started walking briskly away from the fields and headed home. She knew that she was being a coward. Sukhi never tried to revive that fateful encounter and behaved at family events as if no such thing had ever happened.

A similar feeling had erupted within her though when she set her eyes for the first time upon Vikas who was there to briefly visit to his uncle Kesar's house. Vikas looked very fit, without a paunch, unlike most of the boys in her village. His skin, fair and spotless, exuded a glow and his brown eyes were like tiny lakes of intoxicating liquid.

Vikas was clean-shaven and looked like an urban boy, manicured, cultured and sophisticated. Kirti had an insane desire to drink in his whole body. But she was helpless, utterly helpless, and she did not know what to do or how to approach him.

Whenever she visited Uncle Kesar's house, she had her eyes fixed onto the floor in his presence. Words could not be dragged out of her mouth and she remained transfixed, lost in her own subterranean desires. After a week, Vikas went back to his parents in the nearby city and, as time wore on, Kirti forgot the fleeting moments of insanity that had so effortlessly had her whole being in its grip.

"Kirti, get ready and don't take too long. Ranjit is coming soon to meet you. I am making *pakoras*, vegetable fritters." She was jolted out of her trance. "When he is here, I want you to take a glass of masala tea and *pakoras* for him. I can't find the steel tray for that, can you help me find it? It is our family *izzat*, we have to give Ranjit and his uncle, Malkit Singh, a good impression."

The sense of urgency in her mother's voice filled her with a surge of adrenaline and anticipation.

Kirti was surprised that she, too, had a frisson of excitement in her body, even though she was not looking forward to this encounter.

"What if he says 'no' after having seen me? I am not very tall, about 5' 3", with a wheatish complexion. I've no visible blemishes on my face, but my clothes are not always what you could call modern or trendy."

She got her clothes made in the village. Parsa Ram had been their family tailor for many decades. Whenever there was a wedding in their extended family, he would bring his Singer sewing machine to their house and work on making special garments for the family. He had not been to a city for years and didn't know much about the changing fashions in clothes. The clothes he put together were well-made, slightly old-fashioned but, nevertheless, looked good when worn.

Much of Kirti's excitement evaporated when she saw Ranjit. He was slightly chubby, paunchy, with bulging, droopy eyes, a bouffant at the front held together by what seemed to be some kind of a starchy paste. He was wearing blue jeans with several holes around the knees. His uncle, Malkit Singh, was with him, looking equally dishevelled and unkempt. They were sitting in the front of the house on chairs that her father had hastily borrowed from Richa's family.

Kirti brought in a tray laden with steaming glasses of masala tea and a huge pile of *pakoras*. While she was serving tea, Ranjit looked sheepishly, but stealthily at her. She did not enjoy his staring at her. After she had offered *pakoras* on small plates, she went back to the kitchen to let the men have a free conversation. After what seemed like an eternity, her father called her in to join them. She sat, feeling shrunk and withdrawn within herself.

After a pause, Uncle Malkit Singh cleared his throat, caressed his billowing white beard, had another gulp of tea and then proceeded to announce: "Kirti, from now on, you are our *bahu*, our daughter-in-law."

Kirti stole a glance at Ranjit and he had a smile on his face. The smile didn't look very spontaneous and seemed to be somewhat contrived. She didn't have any lightning pass through her body and felt she shouldn't react or show any emotions on hearing this news. She made her excuses and took the aluminium teapot back to the kitchen. Ranjit and Malkit Singh left soon after that and she saw her mother losing no time praying to Waheguru and offering thanks for giving their daughter the opportunity to go to Villayat, England.

3

The time of departure for England, as expected, was very stressful. They had arrived at Amritsar airport in the small hours of the morning, while the dawn was still trying to shake off its sleep. While going towards the airport, Kirti saw many stray dogs rummaging for food through debris outside eating places. There was litter on both sides of the road and Kirti felt forlorn as if she were being banished. Both her mother and father stayed silent much of the time during their journey and whenever they spoke, she could hear only words moistened by their tears. Her brother, Saninder, too, was unusually less noisy and boisterous. He kept talking about the urgency of finding some food at the airport as he was perpetually famished.

Raja Sansi Airport was a small place. After the checking in, she found herself in the waiting lounge where there were a few people resting on seats, some snoring, some lying with their eyes closed, faces covered with assorted bits of fabric.

The whole place had a deserted look, without much hustle and bustle. There was what looked like a tea stall with half a dozen passengers crowding around it for sweet stewed tea and samosas. The stallholder did not seem to welcome brisk trade and his body language and insouciant responses to requests from customers gave the impression that he found the whole thing disruptive and a bit intrusive. But Kirti could not focus on her immediate surroundings. She was thinking of the farewells she'd have to make before disappearing into the cavernous waiting area.

The teary voice of her father, the subdued wailing of her mother and the sudden quiet that had descended on Saninder's face, the invocations to Waheguru and the repeated reminders to do her best to please her new family in England – Kirti's mind was in a whirl. She did not even notice that the waiting area was now bursting at the seams with people booked on the same flight to Birmingham.

The plane took off and Kirti knew it was a plunge into the unknown. The haunting farewells, the final torrent of advice on how she would be expected to behave in her new country and how the honour of the family rested on her shoulders – it was a very strange journey. She did not know anything about the culture or mores of the culture where she was going to set up home. All she knew was that it was very cold, damp and generally miserable.

The whole plane journey was steeped in a fog; she wasn't aware of what food was being served or how the time passed.

There were passengers around who looked excited though. Most were returning home after a visit to the sub-continent and they must have spent a happy time with their parents, siblings or other relatives, Kirti surmised. She knew that the concept of having a holiday for most Indians visiting India was to stay with their relatives and venture out of their villages as little as possible. She had seen many people returning from England to places close to her village who spent most of their time there sitting by the tube wells in their ancestral land and just visiting or receiving other relatives there. Perhaps the stillness, the quiet broken only by the occasional barking of a stray dog or the low decibel noise emanating from the bubbling saucepans in the neighbourhood was an antidote for the hectic life in their new country.

Her mum had knitted a number of cardigans and jumpers and given them to her to shield her from the cold in England.

On landing in Birmingham, she was met by half a dozen people from Ranjit's family: his father, mother, sister, aunt and a wizened old woman who must be, she thought, their granny or one of their elderly relatives. As they came out of the airport, Kirti was surprised to see everything so clean and tidy. There were no piles of dust or garbage as she was used to in India. And there were no roaming cows and buffaloes on or by the roadside. It was cold though, bloody cold, and Kirti could feel the chilly breeze penetrating her bones.

The journey to Ranjit's family home in Oldbury was not that arduous. Although the women from his family were asking Kirti questions about her flight, customs, immigration and unending questions about her family, Kirti was fixated on the motorway they were travelling on at what seemed to be a breakneck speed. The traffic in Phagwara, and other places in the bit of India that she knew, always moved like a snail. A frenetic snail though. The drivers spent much of their time there dodging other vehicles and, even in the early hours in the morning, the vehicles drowned in a cacophony of tooting horns. Although it might seem to be chaotic to an outsider, she, like other people living in India, found security in the random overtaking of vehicles from left, right or from any other direction available. Their van from Birmingham airport was moving at speed, without dodging other vehicles, without the bleeping of its horn and staying in one lane without being tempted by other vacant ones. The road did not pass through any towns or villages and that, too, was a little surprising to Kirti. And there were no people sitting by the roadside, gossiping or passing their time while staring at traffic. Hordes of people in her village took great pleasure in gazing and staring at everything that moved.

The house they arrived at, she discovered later, was a terraced one. On entering, Kirti found it very narrow, like a cage, confined and rather claustrophobic. There was no courtyard; windows had glass panes, instead of a metal grilles.

Her mother-in-law poured some mustard oil on the threshold of the house and put a piece of very sweet *burfi* into Kirti's mouth to welcome her into her family. Ranjit, while trying very hard to smile, did not look very excited. She had a maelstrom of emotions which made her almost giddy. She was surrounded by strangers whom she had met for the first time in her life. "Am I at their mercy?" She could not figure out any sensible answer. The other women, and there were quite a few milling around in the house, took turns to put some money into her *chunni* which she was told to hold tightly with both hands. Some more sweet things, *laddus*, more *burfi* and other confectionery bits were thrust into her mouth.

After this initial baptism of fire was over, Kirti missed the courtyard of her parents' house, its openness, space and freedom. She did not enjoy being the centre of attention either. She was besieged by lots of older women, who were staring and smiling at her and stuffing her mouth with yet more cloying sweets. Sweets used to taste much better in India but here, they only tasted of sugar. She longed to be an ordinary girl, almost anonymous, part of the furniture in the family and she did not enjoy even in the slightest the fuss being made of her. Everything was so formal, ritualised and the whole occasion apparently never-ending. High walls of loneliness were closing in and she felt scared.

The rest of the evening was equally hectic. Ranjit disappeared while rituals were being performed and came back after having a few beers with his friends in the Desi Queen, a local pub. Kirti felt very exposed and vulnerable without her mum and friends. But there was no turning back. She was 5000 miles away from her village in a strange country, surrounded by some very strange people.

The intense feeling of loneliness, thankfully, did not persist beyond the first month or two. Kirti got used to the routine in her new home. She was given a number of things to do every day, "so that you feel at home", as her mother-in-law put it to her. She was tasked to cook food for the whole family, clear the kitchen and wash the dishes and utensils. Since Dalbir, her mother-in-law, proclaimed her complete trust in her ability to be an integral part of the family, she was also asked to make sure all the rooms were cleaned, dusted and polished at least once a week.

"It is important to give you a sense of ownership by looking after the family household," she once said in a matter-of-fact voice. "Ranjit's *papaji* and I are here in this world only for a short while. After we have received a call from Waheguru, it is you who will have to take on the responsibility for this family," Dalbir said in a voice soaked in self-pity. Kirti felt churned within.

She cursed Dalbir under her breath, wishing all sorts of calamities to befall her. "Let her body be riddled with worms and insects. What have I done to deserve this kind of routine? At my parents' house, I did only light jobs, such as making a jug of tea, tidying up my room, putting the washing on the line. Most of my time was given to playing with my friends, doing my homework or making a small talk with visitors to our house."

There used to be a number of regular visitors at her parents' house whose regular appearance was part of the family routine that she'd found reassuring. There was Rajo, the oldest woman in her *mohalla*, or street, who looked shrivelled and slightly bedraggled, but who could charm anyone with her gossip about the other villagers and their families. Her toothless smile and her *dupatta* sliding off her white, threadbare head and the frequent bouts of her small cough were a daily experience that she used to enjoy.

Then there was Bhago, everyone's aunty in the village, who would bring in another sheaf of gossip, rumour and news about local life. Kirti particularly liked the regular visits by Bhago for two reasons. She was exceptionally ugly with furrowed skin, with a mile-long gap between her front teeth and hair which was constantly rebellious. Everyone else in comparison to her looked normal, if not attractive. Secondly, Bhago couldn't keep inside any rumours or news that had come her way in the village. She would tell Kirti's mum anything and everything that anyone had done in the village, including her own daughters-in-law. And she would ask her listeners to keep to themselves everything they heard from her.

Kirti also could not forget the periodical visits by Sarna and his wife, Gurditti. They were local weavers and used to weave *khesis*, rustic cotton blankets for her parents. While drinking *lassi*, they would sit beside her mum and Gurditti used to sing Meera Bai's *Bhajans* in a rich, undulating voice. Meera Bai was an eighteenth-century Hindu mystic who composed some haunting melodies due to her devotion to Krishana. Gurditti's singing was a cascade of mellow, soulful music.

Then they used to have visits, often unannounced, by Kirti's mother's relatives, from her parental side and a similar tranche of motley relatives from her father's ancestral family. Despite these visits, life was peaceful, without any tides of excitement, but, more importantly, without any anxiety. Listening to folk songs on the radio or television was enough to spice things up.

"But this bloody witch is asking me to take on the work for the whole family!"

Kirti could not stop tormenting thoughts swarming in her mind. Could anyone see the justice in her situation?

She soon discovered that Ranjit, too, was a dead loss, a counterfeit coin, a massive disappointment. A burden on this earth, indeed. Kirti felt she was a total failure when it came to understanding his relationship with her. For the first a few months, he was very warm and caring. He would come home after work and bring little presents for her: a bottle of perfume, an ornament for their bedroom or even a box of Indian sweets. But she soon figured out that he was not one to display his emotions. He wouldn't hug or kiss her to signal he was happy to see her. Most of the time, he was reticent, not used to small talk and his face mostly remained without even the slightest hint of expression. He looked rather glum though mostly, seemingly finding even exchanging pleasantries a chore.

She thought she could live with that. She knew her conversation, too, was at times truncated. But her reticence was due to the cultural influences she had inherited from her village society. Girls were supposed to be bashful and tongue-tied to show they had imbibed centuries-old traditions.

But surely Ranjit was born in this country, away from village life in India. Why was he so miserly with his words? Words were used by him only for forgettable utterances, such as "I am off to work now," "I'll be late tonight" and "Did you iron my shirt?"

He would not consider giving up going to pubs with his friends, his 'mates'. He would come back home, sometimes quite late at night, and his mum and dad did not even once ask him to be home early to spend some time with Kirti. She couldn't share her worries with anyone though. She did not want her mum and dad to be consumed with anxiety and uncertainty, so she kept everything from them. Over time, she began to realise that she was not an important member of the family, that she was only a spare part to do chores in the house. She was spending her days smouldering with pain and a deep sense of insecurity.

Ranjit worked in a garage, allegedly, as a motor mechanic, but, in reality, he was a dog's body. He worked strange hours, a mixture of twilight ones, sprinkled with a few stints through the night. When he was on night shifts, he would spend much of his day catching up on sleep and then go out in the evening. During his waking hours through the day, he would exercise in his tiny gym that he had installed in the lean-to shed at the back of his parents' house. Kirti was not welcome in the gym because, according to him, the exercises he was doing there were part of his job.

She gathered that his job at the garage was part-time and that he worked there only three nights most weeks. The rest of the evenings were spent in the company of his friends in pubs or wherever they wanted to have a binge.

"Why don't they mend cars during the day? Why are you working night shifts all the while?"

His response was always opaque, a complete puzzle to her. "It's because it is an all-night garage. They have different staff during the day, too."

His relationship with Kirti was very changeable, like the English weather. Sometimes, he was sweet as *gur*, the solidified molasses that Kirti used to enjoy as her dessert. Sometimes, he was very distant, aloof, avoiding eye-contact with her and showing no inclination to start or respond to any conversation.

One day, he went to Aldi in the high street and brought a cake for Kirti. She was happy and they shared the cake with a cup of masala tea. But this didn't happen often and he wouldn't bring a broken twig for her, let alone a cake or a box of chocolates. His mercurial change of moods struck her as very odd and alarming.

Even though Kirti had come from a village without any first-hand knowledge of love, she knew there was no love or real affection flowing from Ranjit. They were living in the same house, but only as strangers and Ranjit was, at times, a million miles away from her. No amount of housework or doing chores for him was sufficient to thaw his permafrost feelings towards her. Physical intimacy was non-existent too and averting their eyes from each other when in the same room was the norm.

He didn't show a very different face to his mum and dad either. Communicating in grunts, groans, a mumbled yes or an almost inaudible no, with a sulky look in his eyes was his normal fare. On many occasions, the haunted look on his face and his glazed eyes used to scare Kirti. But she was not willing to blame herself for anything that might have precipitated these things in him. She was doing her best to be a good wife and the unrequited affection was corroding her inside. He liked to spend much of his time asleep or playing with some electronic gadget, usually sprawled on his bed in his room. He would leave the house before six in the evening and return home in the early hours of the morning.

Kirti had heard so much about the warmth that flows from a new marriage, how two people shared the narratives of their pre-wedding lives with each other, how they found even an hour's separation unbearable and how they talked and talked about their future plans. But it was very different here. When in bed, they lay on an icy sheet and thick glaciers kept them apart.

Ranjit took her to see an Indian film at Cineworld a couple of times. A few times, he ordered a pizza from Domino's and those little treats made her forget her anguish for a moment or two. But such acts of affection were rare, like the moon at the time of Eid. You had to wait a long time before it came into sight. The house became a dungeon, with a grinding sameness of routine and a corrosive feeling of loneliness with no friend to turn to.

Kirti often recalled the advice given by her mother like a mantra;

"*Beti*, you have to accept a lot of hard work and heartburn when you go to your husband's house, you have to suppress your desires, respect your mother-in-law, even when she is obsessive about sending troubles your way. It is only after those experiences that you can hope to have some happiness. Like gold, you have to go through fire to retain your purity and lustre. If you do not accept pain in the early days, you will lose the plot forever."

All she could think of at such moments was something she knew her mum wouldn't have wanted to hear from her.

"What about my rights? I am being told to embrace troubles, just to please my good-for-nothing husband. Why don't they advise him to do the same? Is he made of gold? Is it because I am a girl and, in the world we live in, girls are inferior to boys?"

Life, untouched by love and affection, went on for several months. Kirti felt she was not well-versed in modern mores; she was not educated enough to understand the subtexts of what people said or did. But she knew that her marriage was a soulless affair. All she got was household chores and the company of her mother-in-law, there was absolutely nothing there to lift her spirits and make her heart beat a little bit faster. She was constantly thinking of a sentence in Punjabi which translates as: "I have a drum around my neck and I have no choice, but to beat it."

She carried a heavy millstone around her neck, a constant

reminder that by coming over to the UK, she had made a big mistake.

Actually, it was not a mistake made by her. Her parents had made the choice for her and, whatever reason they might have for their decision, she was the one who was suffering, having to spend time in dark, hopeless surroundings without any exit. She felt like she was trapped in solitary confinement in Alcatraz, even though she had committed no crime.

She did not even have many friends outside the confines of the house. She could see from her bedroom window or when she was shopping for vegetables at the Indian cornershops that English girls looked carefree, with a spring in their step, wearing trendy clothes and often walking, fingers hooked, with their boyfriends or partners. She felt pangs of envy in her heart when she saw them smiling, talking and sometimes kissing each other. They must have accumulated good karma in their past life to merit such freedom. She felt sure they did not have to worry about their mothers-in-law or attracting any opprobrium from their families or relatives.

She was living in a very black and white environment in which girls transferred from other families through an arranged marriage did not have many rights.

4

Spending a bit of time with Susie was a huge relief to Kirti. Susie was Ranjit's cousin and lived only a couple of miles away. She was just over eighteen and had left school without any qualifications, with no aspirations to get acquainted with higher education. She was biding her time while her parents were busily searching for a boy who could become her husband. The search was taking a long time because there were quite a few hurdles they had to overcome. They wanted a boy who belonged to the same religion, same caste, preferably a businessman and someone who could afford to give their daughter a little bit of luxury in her new home. Susie had a lot of time on her hands as she was not expected to do any chores at home because that was the duty of her sister-in-law, Jaswinder. Also, her mother, Balbir, still continued to cook daily meals for the family.

Susie had a frothy personality, excitable, in love with her own voice. She was of a slight build, with dark brown skin with a heavy layer of foundation on her face. She did not have any school qualifications, but she could speak English like a native and was fond of using the Black Country dialect, which Kirti found impossible to understand. Her real name was Simran, but every one called her Susie. Taking on an English-sounding first name was seen as a sign of being anglicised, of being part of the wider society.

Susie had had flings with a couple of boys at school, but kept her dalliances to herself. She confided in Kirti how she used to bunk off school to be with her boyfriends. Kirti listened to her adventures intently and they sounded like tales from another world. Very bad, but very exciting at the same time. Susie began visiting Kirti at least twice a week and her presence mitigated her sense of loneliness a smidgen.

Kirti did not have much communication with her parents in India. They did not want to seem to be intervening and genuinely did not want to ask her if she was having any difficulties settling down in her new home. They were of the firm view that once a girl left her parents' home, she should focus solely on her new life with her husband and his parents. If Kirti ever talked with them over the telephone that talk very swiftly flitted from topic to topic without touching on anything that could be regarded as personal. It was usually: "How is Ranjit? How is Dalbir? How are Ranjit's sisters? Are you looking after yourself and cooking nice meals for Ranjit and his family?" Kirti felt imprisoned within the thick walls of silence and indifference. Villayat, England, had turned into a curse for her, a place of torment where she found herself pining for freedom, caring people, warmth.

Kirti got a shock one morning when her mother-in-law told her: "Kirti, Ranjit has left home. I don't know when he is coming back. He is not leaving this town, but will live in a different house."

Dalbir spoke in a matter-of-fact tone, but Kirti found the news like a rapier slicing through her heart. She did not expect him to leave home, though they were living parallel lives anyway. He did whatever he wanted to do without discussing anything with her. The very fact that they were living in the same house provided her with some respect within the Punjabi society. Living together under the same roof with or without any closeness or emotional resonance was sufficient for the local community around her.

Love to people around her was something akin to a passing feeling, nothing more than a fleeting bout of lust. Looking after your husband's parental family and performing rituals to please his relatives was what ensured acceptance and respect. Kirti now felt lost. There was no one there she could talk with or share her inner howling. She took a deep breath to share her turmoil with Dalbir while cooking in the kitchen, but her response was very dispiriting. Her anxiety was brushed aside in an unconcerned, perfunctory manner and she said: "Ranjit will come back home soon before long. Young boys often have this kind of wanderlust."

On another occasion, she said: "Kirti, if you had looked

after Ranjit a bit more, he would have not left home."

Kirti went into her room and felt a mix of anger, disgust, sorrow and a soul-destroying premonition of her future.

Days and nights passed and the pain she felt when Ranjit had left her had now become a dull ache, annoying, but something she could cope with. She still had the same questions haunting her though: "Why did he leave me? Why did he not even bother telling me that he was going to desert me? He had never been physically cruel to me, he never raised his voice when speaking to me. He just ignored me! Why, oh, why?"

The pain, however, felt less penetrating after a few months and the restlessness that kept her awake at night, making her feel abandoned and forlorn, incrementally became more acceptable. If he did not treat her as an individual person with some fundamental human rights, why should she worry about him? During one of her telephone calls, she told her parents, but their response was that she should sort things out at her end.

"What can we do while 5,000 miles away from you?"

Susie's mother, Balbir, tried to help her assuage her pain by taking her out to some the social events they attended within their community. She started going to the *gurdwara* with Dalbir and attended various social festivities with her and Balbir.

The visits to the *gurdwara* were not always for listening to the *granthi* recite verses from *Guru Granth Sahib* or losing oneself in the singing of *shabads* by the *raagis* or musicians. Much of the time there was spent exchanging news, maligning "friends" who were not present, whispering rumours about the news from Punjab, plus talk about fashions, prices and the misdemeanours of girls in the neighbourhood.

The women there found the setting very conducive to back-biting, making scathing statements about people from their village, or whoever was the target of criticism on the many ethnic television channels. The frequent visits to the *gurdwara* thus did nothing to replace the malignant agitation afflicting Kirti.

Months passed and she did not get any further news about Ranjit. He did not visit his parents' house while she was there, but would come there only when she was out. Kirti did not have any surge of grief when thinking about his unannounced departure, but she wished she knew why he had decided to desert her. What went wrong to force him to decide to leave home? She could not hold onto anything to explain his sudden decision. Or was it because it was her destiny?

Seasons came and went and even her search for an answer became more and more futile and pointless, losing much of its urgency. Since Kirti did not have any fond memories of Ranjit to plague her lonely hours, she felt more and more reconciled with what had happened. The lingering bitterness, the abrupt ending of their relationship, the unexplained disappearance of Ranjit from her life – it all left Kirti with a desire not to contemplate any future liaisons.

In the first autumn of her loneliness, she was shopping at Bentley Bridge, browsing in Laura Ashley. The sky was overcast, laden with moisture and the signs of impending winter were becoming more and more noticeable. She caught a fleeting glimpse of Ranjit at the corner of her eye, heading towards the B&M shop. She noticed a middle-aged woman walking alongside him.

Sudden feelings of resentment and incomprehension sprang up like Hydra's many heads in her mind.

An irrepressible doubt arose in Kirti's mind as she wondered who that woman was. She was much older than Ranjit and did not exude any grace or beauty. In fact, she was rather flappy and walked with a slight waddle.

When Kirti returned home, she mentioned her surprising sighting of Ranjit and his mysterious companion to Dalbir who, probably giving in to the obvious distress of her questioning, admitted that she had known Ranjit's liaison with Samantha, someone who lived less than a mile from their house. Samantha, she learnt, was a single parent with two children, both at primary school. She didn't know how long Ranjit and Samantha had been together, but they clearly were an item now. While she was wondering where Ranjit had disappeared to, he had been staying with Samantha all the while. She was plump, without a job and had been living in a council house since her previous partner decided to leave her. An obsessive fondness for drink, coupled with the boisterous nature that Samantha was said to have in abundance, made Kirti wonder why and how Ranjit could fancy her.

But at least the mystery of his vanishing from her life was

solved and, somehow, she found that cathartic, despite the periodic eruption of anger and repulsion inside her soul. She was determined not to let this disastrous discovery disrupt her peace for much longer though. She decided to consign Ranjit to the dustbin of her memory. Three years had passed since their wedding and she knew she was able to divorce him and still have a legal entitlement to stay in England.

In spite of her resolve to punish Ranjit for his infidelity for dumping her so unceremoniously, Kirti discovered from time to time that the simmering pain in her soul abruptly emerged to torment her. "Where did I go wrong? Why me?" Or, "I tried to be a good wife, not making any demands on him. What attracted him to Samantha?" She knew the questions haunting her did not have any answers, but she couldn't help going over them in her moments of darkness.

She still had the benign company of Dalbir and her husband, Randhir. They did everything they could to support her, consoling her in her moments of dejection and taking her out on their regular visits to the local *gurdwara*. A sense of guilt and trying to atone for their past indifference perhaps made them more caring and hospitable. Kirti liked cleaning the house and cooking for the three of them. The arrangement suited everyone as Dalbir appreciated the company that she provided and Kirti did not feel any real pangs of loneliness. Perhaps things could go on as they were for a long time. She did not have the courage to envisage a time when the cosy arrangement with Ranjit's parents would come to an end, even though she knew she had the option of divorce.

It was high summer and the sun was blazing in all its glory. Kirti went shopping for food on her own. In the Iceland supermarket at the fringe of the almost deserted high street, there she met Aunty Maninder who was looking for some fresh salad.

"*Sat Sri Akaal*, aunty."

Aunty Maninder hugged Kirti like a long-lost member of her own family. Kirti could feel the warmth of her greeting. She had met Maninder only a few months earlier at a social event which she was attending in the company of Susie's mother, Balbir.

Maninder was full of life, slightly ebullient, with a penchant for talking with other people. She looked well-built, with a face that could burst into a smile at any moment. She was browsing with a concentrated look, scrutinising the nutritional details on packets and bags. Kirti knew from her previous encounters that Maninder had a knack of talking at length with strangers. Even her remarks about the weather or on other peripheral things in daily life sounded genuine, infused with warmth. At their first meeting, Maninder had been given a detailed briefing about Kirti's marital crisis by Balbir who had known her for decades.

Maninder was almost, but not yet quite, sixty, but her movements and conversation belied her age. She was very unlike older people in Kirti's village who were always busy ascribing even minor ailments to their age. They sometimes believed that pretending to be older than their biological age was something to boast about. But Maninder was very modern in her outlook and it soon became obvious to Kirti that she did not have much time for the rituals and formalities straightjacketing relationships in punjabi families. She believed in living life to the full, enjoying the present with an eye on the future.

Maninder's clothes were always elegant, well-made and in a variety of bright, but never loud colours. Her face glowed and her speech was always peppered with wisdom and experience. Even after having lived in England for thirty years or so, Maninder's command of Punjabi colloquialisms was amazingly fresh. She could pour an ocean of meaning into a single half-forgotten punjabi phrase.

Their first meeting was at one of Kirti's distant relatives' house. The event they both were attending reminded Kirti of Punjab as it was entirely without structure, rather chaotic and manic at times but, nevertheless, moved at a very slow pace. The event celebrated some arcane rituals – before her wedding the bride had a mixture of gram flour, turmeric and oil plastered over her face, arms and legs. Samreet who was getting married the following weekend was having this traditional cleansing ceremony performed on her and the women surrounding her took turns to put dabs of the poultice-like mix on her limbs. They were singing some punjabi wedding songs at the same time, strewn with sexual innuendos aimed at the bridegroom's family. Samreet was acquiescent, with her eyes staring at the floor and occasionally smiling at the effervescent crowd around her. It was a ceremony open only to female relatives and friends as men were not allowed in the room to participate or even to watch. It was an occasion for women to express their pent-up emotions and the aridity of their daily lives in the absence of judgemental relations. A collective catharsis of women who routinely languished in marriages which denied them choice and freedom.

Maninder did not take an active part in the ceremony and merely sat observing. From time to time, she would talk to Kirti who knew she was trying to make her feel comfortable. Kirti liked Maninder a lot. She could feel warmth flowing towards her through her words and body language.

The members of Ranjit's extended family often regarded Kirti as someone who was not very sociable, as one without any real desire to open up and communicate with them about her anguish or bewilderment or whether she was missing Ranjit. But with Maninder, she felt different. She felt she could talk to her without worrying about her attracting any pre-conceived pronouncements. She began to regard her as her favourite aunt, as someone she could trust and confide in.

Even though Ranjit had disappeared from her life, his parents still took it upon themselves to look after her. She had found a job in a factory and worked an afternoon shift most days. On coming home from work, she would find Dalbir and her father-in-law, Randhir, waiting for her. After their evening meal, they would sit with her and whenever she couldn't stop tears rolling down her cheeks, they would try to console her and pledge their support.

Maninder invited Kirti to her house where she lived about five miles away. Her face was not ravaged by any furrows or wrinkles and it was clear to her that Maninder had had a good married life in this country. Her black eyes were bright like shimmering dark pools. Even though Kirti's situation was not news to her, she was still baffled by Ranjit's sudden decision to desert her without giving any clear rationale or premonition. Kirti felt comfortable talking about her predicament with her, although she was still reluctant to share with Maninder her disorienting, unrelenting confusion.

Maninder was very hospitable and addressed her as if she were her own daughter. They sat in her conservatory looking out on the garden while drinking masala tea. The garden was lush, with sharply carved edges, a huge variety of flowers and shrubs in its borders and pink blossom on two trees at the bottom. There was a large patio, immaculately clean, probably freshly slabbed over, and about half a dozen pots adorned with geraniums, begonias and dahlias.

It was so peaceful in the conservatory, even though her house was not very far from the maddening crowds. The sun streaming through the roof and windows was helping Kirti's sentences to be less disjointed. She felt at home; it was the first time someone was so engaging, spurring her to talk about her predicament. She knew full well that Maninder would not be able to do anything to change her situation, but her readiness to listen to her was a real tonic. Kirti cried, sobbed, laughed, talked and listened on her first visit to Aunty Maninder's house.

5

Although my name is Maninder, I used to be called Guddi, a doll, perhaps because I was the youngest in the family and the shortest.

I come from a simple family, the true salt of the earth, with a firm belief in working hard, taking care of their children and being considerate to all. Despite the cataclysmic upheaval that my parents and siblings were forced to go through when India was partitioned in 1947, they set about rebuilding their lives in Rawal Pindi, a small hamlet in the Punjab.

Sometimes their faces were unlit by smiles, but their dedication to their family was single-minded as ever.

I was only three years old when the traumatic exodus from our ancestral home in Pakistan happened, following the family decision that we would seek security across the border in India. We were allocated a dilapidated house in the Rawal Pindi once we arrived, after a journey that witnessed unspeakable brutalities committed in the name of religion. The enforced migration has remained as a hazy fog in my memory. But I remember the leaking roof of our new house, the incessant monsoons and how we used to be herded into the house of a hospitable neighbour who had a roof that could withstand the fury of these torrential rains.

I was oblivious to the sudden seismic events my parents and brothers had to go through to survive. I was busy playing with other girls in the village and did not observe any startling or inexplicable changes in my parents. They still carried on building a new life without complaining about the sudden lightning that had stuck them. I had a vague idea that, whereas in our previous house in what was now called Pakistan, there was lots of traditional furniture, such as charpoys, chairs, stools, beds and a huge variety of saucepans in the kitchen, in our new house there were empty spaces staring at us in the kitchen and the bedrooms.

I did not, at that time, comprehend the enormous grief consuming my mum and dad.

When I was a teenager, a burning desire was to continue my studies after my matriculation examination in high school. The school had given me a fleeting glimpse of what lay ahead for those who went to college.

There were very few girls from my village who had gone to university as most of them ended up getting married within a few years of leaving school. It was expected that during the transition between leaving school and getting married they would learn how to cook, sew and generally look after the house to "feel settled" in their marital home.

Arranged marriages were the norm and almost everyone I knew in my village followed the same well-trodden path without making any protest.

"Maninder, love is a feeling that really exists, but not here in our rural Punjabi society," my best friend, Kashmir, once explained to me. "Love is all right if it is cocooned within a song or poem. Once let loose, it is the genie out of a bottle, best to be avoided like the plague. My cousin, Anita, in Ludhiana has also told me that falling in love is like swimming across a river of fire. It is exciting, but very dangerous and scalding. Anita has fallen in love with someone who is from the local men's college in the Civil Lines. She says she feels inebriated whenever she thinks of her boyfriend. She is frightened to mention her relationship to her parents."

I looked at Kashmir wide-eyed as if listening to a folk tale about fairies and jinns.

Kashmir also often talked about another cousin who had gone to university and who, after graduation, had found a job in Chandigarh.

"Maninder, Seema is living alone in an apartment in the city. Independent, completely independent! She doesn't have to ask for permission if she wants to go shopping or to ask what to cook or if she can go to the cinema or spend time with friends at weekends."

I could distinctly hear a sigh in her tone. It all sounded

unreal to me, a through-the-looking glass experience, a glimpse of another parallel universe. It made me immerse myself in the poetry of Amrita Pritam, Sahir Ludhianivi and listen more intently to the timbre and undertones of folk songs.

I was an above average student with an intense desire to have the wings to fly and enjoy the blue skies that higher education represented.

A bit of courage was all I needed. Who to approach and what to say was something intractable for me. I had boundless love from my mum and dad, but there was no mention of any career or education for me. I was the youngest in the family and I felt everyone thought that lavishing physical care on me alone would be enough to support my well-being.

My parents had a sizeable piece of arable land in my ancestral village which was pronounced to be part of Pakistan after partition. The arbitrary Redcliff line had been drawn on the map in August 1947 and the new borders of the two new countries became part of the sub-continent's map. My parents had to leave their farm and head to India, leaving all their assets behind. When I became a little older, it began to make sense to me that my parents were trying hard to rebuild their shattered lives from a very low level. But, at that time, austerity, unfamiliar hardships, scarcity of resources and the empty, bareness of the house in our new surroundings – it was new to me, but I was so busy with the present without any memories of the comfortable past haunting me. I made friends in Rawal Pindi, spent a lot of time playing with girls in the neighbourhood and felt secure in the love of my mum and dad.

I was the only girl child in the family. There were four older brothers, but I received special favours from my mum. Usually in the rural parts of India, boys are regarded as the treasure of the family, guaranteeing continuity of the family name for generations to come. They are also seen as the main carers for ageing parents. Girls traditionally go to stay with their in-laws and, in time, transfer their familial allegiance to their husbands' family.

There had been a drought of girls in my parents' family and, after the successive births of four brothers, my mum and dad were yearning to have a daughter. My arrival was, therefore, warmly greeted. I understand that after my birth, sweets were distributed in the village to mark the momentous family occasion. I was singled out for special attention, not only from my parents, but also from my older brothers. Copious amounts of milk, buttermilk, *parathas*, and makeshift toys filled my time. Although I do not have very many discrete memories of what happened in my family home in my early days, I still remember the snippets of advice my mum used to give me for my protection.

My mum used to say in wistful, almost semi-moist tones to me from time to time: "Maninder, I wish I could give you the moon and stars, but, *beta*, my daughter, I am helpless, I do not have anything worthwhile to give you except my love. May Waheguru give you happiness all through your life!"

I went to a primary school in the neighbouring town Garhshankar, a distance of just over a mile from home. Garhshankar seemed to be an enormous city to me, with scores of shops in its bazaar, all busy with customers from surrounding villages and many local curious window-shoppers whose pastime it was to browse without having to spend any money. The throngs of people, passers-by and what seemed to be a hectic pace of life there used to fill me with awe and wonder. I used to be overwhelmed by the range of activities taking place: an annual fair, a festival to celebrate Lord Shiva's birthday and the periodic visit from a touring circus.

For the first four years of my schooling, my dad used to take me to school and fetch me from there every day. He was taciturn by nature, not given to much talking, but everything he did was bathed in warmth and dignity. The expression on his face and the sparkle in his eyes spoke volumes of his affection towards me. He had a white beard, with unruly hair he had tamed well. I always saw him wearing a turban, white, gingerly starched most days, except when attending a marriage when he would go for a more sober colour. He wore immaculately clean clothes, made of simple, rustic fabrics, with a tunic and pyjama bottoms, as was the norm in villages. He had a wheatish complexion and his hands had protruding veins which had a bluish tinge. Much of his conversation with me was through his smiles. I enjoyed his mostly silent company.

At the end of the school day, I used to wait eagerly to see him and his unfurling smile. He would take my satchel, so that

47

I could cover the distance home in skipping jumps.

In my fourth year at school, my mum took over the responsibility of escorting me to and from school. Not far from my school gates, there was a narrow canal which had a bridge built over it for pedestrians to cross to the other side. At the end of the school day, I used to feel a gentle wave of excitement lapping up against the inside of my body. The sight of my mum standing there with her gaze fixed on the school gate used to fill my heart with waltzing joy.

One of my brothers, Surjit, got engaged to a girl in Garhshanker. The girl lived there with her parents, slightly away from the town centre. That suburb was quite small, often smothered in the exhaust fumes of passing lorries and the other traffic which passed through it as a short cut to get to Hoshiarpur. It had a bustling market where vendors used to try to coax potential customers to purchase their wares, such as vegetables, assorted seasonal fruits, cheap make-up, creams, lotions and lipsticks and various haberdashery items. To me, that part of the town, though only half a mile away from my school, looked gigantic, exciting, inviting further exploration.

One day my mum was slightly late and I took that opportunity to visit my brother's would-be-bride. When my mother arrived and stood on the canal bridge with her eyes fixed on the school gate, she was so distraught when she could not see me. She asked everyone she met tearful questions. After some time, my would-be sister-in-law's mother asked me if I had informed my mum about my visit to their house straight after school. When I shook my head, she took me back to the school and there was my mum standing there, driven insane by worry and, when she caught a glimpse of me, she ran towards me and clasped me to her chest, showering me with countless kisses interspersed with a telling off.

The school I attended was a typical Indian school, without many resources, staffed by indifferent teachers, and, all in all, a dreary place, not stimulating, even for the stray dogs roaming around its periphery. When I was nine years old, we were sitting on the floor on the roof of one of the two classrooms designated for classes to move through on a rota basis. Those who were waiting for their turn sat under trees on jute sacks in a nearby mango garden. We were listening to the teacher who had asked us to listen to her exposition without interrupting her. Asking questions or seeking clarifications was not something that endeared you to your teachers. As a general rule, they liked their students to listen to them in silence and execute their instructions when setting follow-up work.

Our teacher, Partap Kaur, was explaining something about science. She had a distinctly aggressive dislike of girls asking her questions. If what she said did not make sense, so what? We needed to do our own research. It was disrespectful to ask questions during lessons anyway, she used to insist. We were pretending to be listening to her intently on that fateful sunny afternoon. The monsoons had come and gone and, at the onset of winter, the temperature was more temperate than at the height of summer. In order to keep the slight chill at bay, we were enjoying the warmth caressing the air around us, oblivious to what Mrs Kaur was saying.

Suddenly, there was a discombobulating noise, a loud thud and then we felt the ground had opened up underneath our feet. Soon we realised that the flat roof of the classroom where our lesson was taking place had collapsed. Many of the girls, including me, went down with the falling debris, landing on the ground floor underneath. I was covered in dust and, while still in a daze, came to realise that I was bleeding. I blinked in the blazing sun, stood up, wiped my eyes with my hands and walked out of the debris heading towards the playing fields a few metres away. I had no inkling as to what had happened. As soon as I reached the playing fields, I collapsed and lost consciousness.

When I opened my eyes, I found myself in the civil hospital in Garhshankar, with my mother sitting at the bottom end of my hospital bed. Her face was frozen with terror.

As I came around, I sat up in my bed, leant forward, wiped the tears from her eyes and said, "*Beji*, please do not worry, I am all right. It was not a big accident; I am okay, don't worry."

It took me almost two months to recover from that accident. I was due to sit a scholarship examination to try to win a paid place for my middle school years, but now I had to forego my aspirations and, instead, sit only the in-house annual examinations at my school.

Something very minor, of apparently little significance, happened one morning though and I found my formative years impacted in an unforeseen way.

"Maninder, can you get up and sweep this corner of the courtyard?" I half-heard what my mum had said while I was drifting in and out of sleep. I was lying on my charpoy in the courtyard as the sun was blazing across the cloudless sky. I didn't feel like getting up and let any sleep-wrecking work disrupt my morning.

"Maninder, did you hear what I said to you ten minutes ago? The sun is half-way across the sky and you are still asleep. Don't you have any agility left in your body to wake up and do your bit?" intoned my mum beseechingly, but with a nagging persistence.

I got out of bed, swept my corner of the courtyard, chucked the rubbish I had collected onto the bit of vacant land over the boundary wall. Then I went in and had a look in the ancient freckly mirror that still clung to the wall by the door in my room. I had a good look at my figure and came to the painful conclusion that perhaps I was too chubby to be agile, too fat to do anything with alacrity. I did not feel nimble; I felt I was heavy, bordering on being obese. I had to do something urgent to redress it and get back to being a normal girl of fourteen. The only solution was not to eat normal portions of food, but that was bound to cause a lot of argument in the family as we used to eat outside in the courtyard and could not hide smaller food portions.

I longed to be a perfect girl – stout but not chubby, strong, but not flabby. I had seen pictures of Bollywood actresses in magazines and I yearned to be like them, slim, without any fat sticking around the periphery of my body. Some of these models and actresses did not do any dieting or vigorous workouts. At least this is what I thought. I hated them for being so 'normal'.

I became obsessed by an intense desire to lose weight and the only course of action open to me, so I thought, was to regularly purge in the communal bathroom after every mealtime. I knew I was inflicting pain on myself by forcing myself to throw up, but I felt I had to make sacrifices to achieve my goal. I invented brazen lies and hid my obsession from my parents.

With hindsight, I am glad I did not allow my bulimia to degenerate into a full-blown anorexia. The long spell of confusion about being 'normal' lasted beyond my teenage years and even after I had come over to England for my marriage, I found the practice of throwing up in secret somehow comforting. Gradually though, I regained my confidence after several years, but the wariness about my food intake lasted at least two decades during which I did my best to eat and drink only low fat foods.

The pendulum swung in the opposite direction when twenty years into my marriage when I began gorging on cakes, pastries and biscuits. Not in addition to my main meals, but in place of them. After a hard day's work, I used to come home from Stourbridge without even an ounce of energy left in my exhausted body. Whatever I found in the cupboard, be it a piece of cake, a pastry or two or even stale remnants of food from the previous night, I would devour them and then slouch down on the sofa feeling listless, completely devoid of energy.

The fact that I started suffering from hypertension did not help matters either.

I was living for my family and what I needed for my body and mind was not deemed by me to be a priority. The accumulation of junk food in my bloodstream did not do much to improve my high blood pressure and one of the consequences was that I became more and more tense, prone to getting irritated over minor, insignificant incidents and increasingly open to onslaughts of obsessive, depressing anxieties.

Anyway, back to the time when marriage had not entered my thinking, when, after matriculation, I sought admission to a girls' college in the small town of Sidhwan. The admission was an accident. A happy accident, I must add. My mum and dad wanted me to do a course in sewing and embroidery because those skills were, and still are, much sought-after in many households in rural Punjab. After cooking and cleaning, sewing was an attribute much valued by people, particularly older members of a family. Sheena, my older cousin, took me to a woman called Harmeet who was giving tutorials in sewing clothes.

Harmeet looked very stern and daunting to me, being loud in her admonishments of the students sitting on the floor of a room that had not seen much sunlight for aeons. They were sitting on burlap sacks, bent over their pieces of fabric with sewing needles poised. Some girls were frantically trying to sew bits of fabrics on a few ancient Singer sewing machines. Harmeet was sitting on a large cushion in front of the class with her massive eyes instilling a chill in the poor souls before her. She was not somebody I fancied working with. My reluctance and horrified look made my cousin take me outside where I said: "*Bhenji*, I don't want to attend any lessons here, even if she were dead."

Sheena took me outside the room and tried to convince me that learning to sew would stand me in good stead after marriage and how I would fulfil my parents' wishes by agreeing to swallow the bitter pill of my qualms.

I was, nevertheless, determined to seek admission to a college and eventually gain the qualifications to find an office job. Sheena had spent four years in a college in Jalandhar and, to my utter relief, understood the intensity of my desire for further education. She was persuaded to take me to the girl's college instead where I managed to secure admission after an informal interview with the principal. I enrolled as an undergraduate at Khalsa College for Women in Sidhwan Khurd, which was only a few miles away from that terrifying sewing workshop.

My excitement at being able to join a college did not let my feet touch the ground for days. Somehow, I persuaded myself to believe that I would be able to convince my parents that I had made the right choice. They might even give me a pat on the back for taking this bold step. I would be the first girl from my village to have gone into higher education.

When we returned to Rawal Pindi, my parents, to my great relief, did not find anything wrong with my decision and their considerate reaction filled me with an unexpected thrill.

"Maninder, we are happy with whatever you've decided to do."

My mother's words were molten gold. I decided to plunge into my studies with even more determination.

Though I was a quiet student, not given to raucous laughter and gossiping, I enjoyed the first year at the college enormously. The college was in a small village, but had a reputation for good discipline and strict supervision. It had a well-earned reputation for its sports facilities and the quality of pastoral support given to students. There was not much to see in the village: only fields, clusters of houses of various shapes and sizes, a cow or a buffalo outside each house and the usual stray dogs busily rummaging for food.

During my first year there, most of the girls did not have any opportunity to venture out to experience what the village had to offer. I made many friends who provided the background to my life for many, many years to come. Ajit, Harjit and Gauri were the three girls who were my antidote to loneliness; they filled our free time with laughter, talking, joking and reminiscing. They became my lifelong friends, even when physically we were all scattered all over, in India and abroad.

One sunny morning, Mrs Kalra, my English tutor, had a young man with her when she arrived to teach our class. The young man was impeccably dressed in a blue suit, with dreamy eyes behind his glasses and coiffured hair. She introduced him to our class and said that her brother, Shivraj, had just completed his post-graduate course at Chandigarh and was due to start his first job as a lecturer in Patiala. My heart missed a heartbeat when I saw him, but I tried to concentrate on the appropriate use of prepositions as explained by Mrs Kalra.

The very next day, I bumped into Shivraj outside the college tuck shop. He was very warm in greeting me with a *Sat Sri Akaal* and did not avert his eyes even once during that brief encounter. "I would love to spend some time with you," he said before I went into my history lesson.

His thoughts, his face, his looks filled my mind that evening, but I could not think of any possible opportunity to get to know him better. He went back after a couple of days and soon all that was left was a passing memory. That memory resurfaced from time to time in years to come followed by "What if …"

Before the first year was out though, my dream of completing my studies was shattered.

My father had suffered a sudden stroke with an unforeseen, devastating impact on his memory and recall. I found out later that on waking up, he found it difficult to walk steadily, or talk coherently. There were no diagnostic medical tests routinely administered in India at that time and particularly in the isolated hinterlands of Punjab. The incident caught everyone off guard and triggered a huge amount of panic and stress. My father regained his mobility incrementally over the coming months, but the sudden onslaught of a stroke left him half the man he used to be. He became withdrawn and lost his confidence to take on responsibilities for day-to-day chores, such as looking after the family's needs or the daily task of ensuring tenants were working well on his land. The glow of his face deserted him and his look suddenly became forlorn, hauntingly disconsolate.

As I was the only daughter, he was anxious to marry me off as soon as possible so that the additional worry of finding a suitable match for me did not exacerbate his anxieties for the future.

He did not want my brothers to be responsible for arranging a marriage for me either. He had made up his mind that it was his duty, his karma, to make sure I was comfortably ensconced in my new home. The abrupt ending of my dream of attending the college shook me to the core. All the pining for higher education, the dream of being the first girl from my village to have gone to university and the intense desire to have a professional qualification for a career evanesced right in front of my eyes.

Although I understood my father's anxiety about getting me married off while he was still alive, I wailed in silence before extinguishing my dreams for my future. The desire for educational qualifications stayed with me for years, but eventually sank without a trace after marriage.

I was considered to be the right marriage material and feelers were sent out to various relatives and family friends to seek a match for me. A messy task it was indeed, which caused within my tormented heart a lot of turmoil and uncertainty.

My parents readily agreed when a proposal came from a distant relative concerning a young man who was a stock controller in a manufacturing company in Dudley. Although the ancestral village he came from was known for a baffling variety of anti-social behaviour, Harbans Kaur, the go-between assured us that this particular young man was of a gentle disposition, caring attitude and was very unlike the other members of his parental family. Above all it was claimed that he was well-off as he had a steady job.

"He can stand on his two feet and provide you with food and shelter," my mother added in a reassuring tone.

My parents invited him to come over to India to meet with me face-to-face. He came to our village and a pre-engagement agreement, *karmai*, was marked. He did not see me, let alone talk with me. Nor did I catch a glimpse of him. I trusted my parents to have a sound judgement in this matter, but my trust was largely based on my loyalty to family traditions.

My fiancé, Amarjit Singh, had made a special journey to India and had only two weeks off work.

The usual chorus of wedding songs from a brass band and the arrival of crowds of relatives preceded the wedding party. My parents, despite their financial predicament since my father's stroke, did their best to put together striking hospitality and the customary dowry for the wedding. Enormous amounts of food, some exotic, alongside staple items, were cooked in the courtyard of our house. There was a cook in charge of preparing this and he had his stove with masses of burning logs underneath and huge bubbling cauldrons in one corner of our courtyard.

After the religious ceremony was over, I went to my husband's village in the evening. My slight excitement was tinged with a discomforting awareness that a mob of women there were staring at me and saying things which I did not fully comprehend. Perhaps they were trying to make me feel at home after the unhinging, abrupt transition from the familiarity of my parents' home. Within a couple of days after the wedding, Amarjit got ready to return to his job in Dudley, assuring me that he would sponsor my travel to England without delay.

Anxiety, apprehension and a heavy cloud of uncertainty overwhelmed my sense of relief when I landed in London. My husband had booked a flight for me from London to Birmingham and I was coming from Punjab where the sun, even during January, can be, and is, often hot. But in London, there was frozen snow piled against pavement kerbs, the sky threatening to offload a lot more.

6

Arriving in England evoked mixed feelings within me – a melange of wonder, awe, excitement, and fear.

As soon as I landed at Heathrow and cleared customs and caught the connecting flight to Birmingham, I knew that my new homeland was going to be a very cold place. While going through immigration and proceeding towards the hall where custom officers stood weighing up whether they should stop you or let you pass, I caught sight of snow and ice on the pavements. In India, the sun exuded heat during the day even in winter, but in London the sun seemed to have been totally banished and a blanket of greyness spread over pavements guarding the ice against any accidental thaw. I cleared the customs and managed to catch the domestic flight to Birmingham with support from the airline staff.

Outside the Birmingham airport, the leaden sky was finding it difficult to hold on to the water it had sucked out of oceans, lakes, rivers and puddles.

The weather in the middle of January was chilling my bones. I looked at my watch and a sudden panic gripped me when I realised the time Amarjit had said he would be at the airport had long gone. I had missed the arrival time that I had been told by my travel agent. My brothers had communicated that time to Amarjit. What was I going to do?

Despite the busyness surrounding me, I felt helpless. I didn't have access to a telephone; I was feeling hot and unwell, despite the freezing conditions outside the terminal.

To my utter relief and a bit of delight, as soon as I came out of the terminal, I saw Amarjit standing there. He was with his cousin, Gurmel, and had brought fruit, cakes and a few *parathas* to sustain me through the motorway journey.

When, in a shaking voice, I tried to apologise for my lateness, he assured me that my flight was on time. When Gurmel mentioned the five and a half hours' difference between Indian and British times, I knew that I had forgotten to factor that in. I didn't raise that issue throughout the car journey lest I should give them the impression that I was an ignorant girl from a village, unaware of different time zones.

When I had stayed in Delhi the evening before my departure, there was a large demonstration near Janpath with people shouting slogans. Hindi had been declared as the official language of India and there were similar protests taking place in many states in the country. The central government had to give in to their demands and made Hindi one of the official twenty-three languages of the country. The image imprinted on my mind was one of a large numbers of demonstrators, waving homemade flags in a frenzied, demented way. In Birmingham, I found no such noise, no hustle and bustle, no frenetic slogan-raising crowds. It felt so calm as if I was in a different world.

The motorway was wide, with cars and vehicles rushing by on all lanes. I expected a stray cow or two to appear on the motorway, or squatting near the central reservation, but everything seemed to be very orderly and disciplined. The motorway did not pass through any towns or villages as was the norm in India. I was used to waiting at unmanned railway crossings where a barrier would come down when a train was due to pass. A lot of time was spent waiting for the barrier to go up or negotiate your way through the gridlock of traffic. It was, nevertheless, fun and in a way routine.

But the motorway from Birmingham to Dudley was a quiet affair, almost silent and the Vauxhall Corolla we were in sped through the distance at great speed.

Amarjit and I sat in the back seat of the car and I saw him stealing a furtive glance at me. I knew it was not the done thing for a punjabi husband to look at his new bride with affection in the presence of relatives or when out in public. Everything had to be done in privacy. Even in privacy, there was never a sense of abandonment, or any clear affirmation of joy or desire for love. When I got out of the car outside his house, I could feel the freezing wind penetrating every part of my body.

I was relieved when I saw an electric heater with two glowing bars in the front room.

There were a few old women there in the room being giggly and generally raucous, staring at my face and offering me one pound notes as a *shagun*, an offering. In the other living room, there were half a dozen men, Amarjit's relatives or friends and acquaintances from his village in Punjab, downing a glass of whisky to celebrate the occasion. I was exhausted, but to my relief, I found Amarjit's presence and glances reassuring.

I knew that I had to make every effort to make the two-up, two-down house I was in my home. Amarjit, to my utter relief, turned out to be caring and willing to do anything to comfort me to get over the pain of leaving my parental family thousands of miles away.

On his days off work, he would take me to Beatties and buy me clothes or ornaments for the house. Beatties in the Churchill precinct had rows and rows of merchandise that I had never come across in India.

The shops in Nawanshahr or Phagwara were microscopic in comparison and the range of goods on offer were very limited. The shopkeepers did not believe in spending money on lighting or ceiling fans to make shoppers comfortable and relaxed. Much of the shopping was done at lightning speed, targeted, with the shopkeeper or one of their employees following you around. But here in Beatties, it was a different world. The sales staff were polite and did not mind guiding you to the wares you wanted to find. What's more, they provided service with a smile, an unheard-of experience in towns near the *pind* that I had left behind in India.

It didn't take me long to get to know my new neighbours. Next door to us lived an African-Caribbean family. David worked in the local steelworks as a gardener, looking after the lawns there. He was a carefree person, prone to frequent bouts of subdued laughter, who enjoyed talking at length, much of which was in patois which I didn't understand at all.

His wife, Sheila, looked after their little boy who was still in a pram. She was a stern lady and believed that young children had ears on their back and would hear only when smacked.

Once Emmanuel, their boy, was crying so loud, screaming in pain that I couldn't resist crossing over to their garden, taking the little boy in my arms and making soothing noises to console him. Sheila was bellowing and I got the impression she was still rebuking Emmanuel for something he had or hadn't done. Again, I did not fully understand what she was saying, but I knew that she did not resent my intervention.

Opposite our terraced house lived Surjit and his family. Surjit looked ancient to me and he was on a sort of permanent sick leave from the steelworks where he used to work at the blast furnace. His beard was always slightly rebellious with tufts of hair hanging out, his turban askew, somewhat precariously perched on his head and there was a wide gap between his teeth. His two daughters, Sharan and Gauri, seemed to be quite modern, speaking English fluently and wearing Western clothes. Surjit spent much of his time at the local *gurdwara*, helping in the communal kitchen or cleaning floors and neatening the cotton sheets which covered the flowery carpet for the congregation to sit on during worship and prayers. I knew them fairly well, but our relationship was only limited to saying, "Hello," or "How are you?" or exchanging similar pleasantries. Before the first year after my arrival was over, Sharan eloped with a Muslim boy and was never seen again. There was a huge amount of brouhaha in whispers going on within the local Punjabi community and Surjit began to spend even more time at the *gurdwara*.

I made some friends in the street – newly arrived brides or one or two old women who had already decided to dispense advice to me generously and provide their own version of knowledge of the local Punjabi society. I used to have a visit by at least one neighbour each day who would share gossip and narratives of woe with me with much gusto.

Simi was a newly arrived bride who lived a few doors down. Like most of the newcomers in the country, she had arrived with her eyes full of dreams of a better life. She had high expectations about living here being more salubrious than her existence in her parental village. She was hardly over eighteen with a slender frame and had a look of vulnerability about her. An average girl, slightly naïve, bewildered, out of her depth and too afraid to share her anxieties with anyone. Her husband, Tom, had gone over to India to consent to the matrimonial proposal actively promoted by his Uncle Satnam. It was quite common for Indian men to take on English-sounding names to seek acceptability by their white colleagues and neighbours. Tom found Simi pleasant and, within a couple of weeks, got married to her.

The whole of Phillour, her village, was filled with the loud music of a brass band, along with a continuous stream of Bhangra blaring from loudspeakers. All the people in the people collaborated to support Simi's parents because she was regarded as the daughter of the entire village. The fact that she was going to emigrate to England after her wedding lent a sense of urgency to their efforts to ensure all the ceremonies were conducted in style.

The chairs and tables for the fifty odd members of the wedding party were lent by other villagers. The different heights and styles of the furniture assembled thus looked interesting, to put it mildly. Half a dozen neighbours acted as waiters while serving the home-cooked dishes to the guests. A group of women sang various songs, albeit not always in unison.

Her parents had spent a good amount of money putting together a dowry. There was a generous display of the usual emotions commonly observed at Indian weddings when the parents of the bride feel it is their duty to cry their hearts out at the departure of their daughter. Heart-rending emotions become irrepressible for mothers.

A couple of months after her wedding, Simi arrived at Birmingham airport to join Tom in Dudley. Within a few days, she noticed that he was deliberately trying to avoid spending time with her. Months merged into years and she gave birth to two children, a boy and a girl.

It was only after more than five years into her marriage that she discovered that Tom was living with a white woman in another part of the town.

What she found gut-wrenching was that while he was living a life of infidelity, his brother, John, was actively in cahoots with him. Tom's white partner used to visit his parents' house where Simi was living and John used to introduce his brother's secret partner as his girlfriend. Tom and this woman already had a couple of children from their illicit union. Once Simi found out that she was being deceived on such a monstrous scale, she decided to leave and went into a council house.

Over the years, I lost contact with her, but her forlorn face and teary eyes often haunted me in my lonely moments.

We had a constant stream of visitors to the house though. There were many people from Amarjit's village who had settled in Dudley and they thought it was one of their duties to visit us, or the menfolk to go to the local pub and drink copious amount of whisky on return from the bar before wolfing down their food. I used to wonder why they did not like vegetables in their meals, as all pounced on chicken and lamb like famished predators. Perhaps they regarded it as a sign of their newfound prosperity to be able to have meat so often.

What galled me was the long hours they used to spend in our front room, laughing and ruminating about the life in the village they had left behind. Amarjit used to join in, but was more restrained in his consumption of alcohol.

Then there were people from the village who were

newcomers to Dudley. A few would come to our house and stay for ages until they found their own accommodation. In some cases, it would take almost a year before they were able to move out. I had to do their cooking and wash their clothes. I was fuming inside about what I regarded as unnecessary additional workload, but I smothered my angst, not sharing it with Amarjit. In arranged marriages, I was aware that one had to walk on shards of glass sometimes. After a few years, Amarjit got tired of losing his privacy or probably he read the subtext of my body language and the number of visitors and semi-squatters became fewer and fewer.

One evening while we were sitting down watching television to unwind, there were a lot of comments being made about an MP from our neighbouring town, Wolverhampton. Enoch Powell had made a speech predicting that immigrants, particularly black and brown ones, though he did not directly mention their colour, if allowed into the country without any strict border controls would create riots and rivers of blood would flow in some parts of the country. The effect of his speech, though not very evident to us at the time, marked the onset of a long period of hostility towards any newcomers in factories and other workplaces.

I noticed that many of my white colleagues at the factory, where after a restful few months I'd sought a job, underwent a sudden change of attitude towards the black and brown staff there.

This change was reflected in their body language, in the

incidental remarks made about immigration and the new proclivity to constantly devalue other cultures. Some of them thought we had been all living in huts or even trees before moving to England, that we had come from primitive tribes and, above all, that we all came from the same inferior stock. It was very damaging to our self-respect and it took years to recover from.

Months after that 'river of blood' speech, I got a job in a factory in Halesowen and I noticed change in a colleague.

Barbara was cold and rather distant when asking me to pay more attention to detail while inspecting the tiny parts which went into the hi-fis manufactured there. She used to be very friendly with me, asking me about my family or giving me the latest news about her own. The latest present she had received from Keith, her partner, and the travails of looking after a teenager son who had suddenly developed an attitude overflowing with angst – we used to have a good chinwag before starting work.

But after that infamous speech, I felt her looks were frosty, her conversation had dried up and the moment she addressed me, the smile that I was so familiar with evaporated. My Asian co-workers and I felt the same deterioration in behaviour in the marketplace too, with stallholders often not acknowledging what we said. It was clear that we were sometimes unseen to many people around us.

There were many, many female colleagues who remained unaffected by the vitriol of that speech and their desire to mingle with their black and Asian colleagues remained undimmed. Their civility, warmth and friendliness kept my faith in British values. At the other extreme, there was another colleague, my team leader as it happened, who persistently held onto the view that all non-white people had to be invisible. She consistently refused to acknowledge the presence of minority ethnic colleagues. She made no eye contact, not even giving a nod of her head, or a smile – absolutely nothing.

Amarjit had come across a few hostile incidents, particularly when travelling on the bus along his usual work route from Dudley to Wolverhampton.

On one occasion, a yob spat at the bus conductor when he refused to stop the bus to let him get off near his street. Amarjit used to get upset, but he knew that such incidents were very common and mild in comparison with what some newcomers had to contend with.

Thinking about those times, I was a newcomer in this country, but I had a desire to find out, little by little, about the culture, traditions and way of life here. Amarjit's co-villagers or relatives when they were inebriated talked of only what used to go on back in their villages. They would spend hours talking about the cows and buffaloes and the people they had left behind in a nostalgic way.

My mother-in-law, Jagiro, came over from India while en route to Canada to stay with her daughter, Jeeto. She was a shrivelled old woman, with millions of furrows on her face and noxious words tumbling out of her mouth. Smiles had never come close to her lips and her stare was so penetrating that it would have scared even members of Dracula's family. During her one month stay with us, she did not condescend to do anything for anyone in the house, refusing to even make a cup of tea for her own son. With a fixed growl on her face, she used to sit and give me the shudders with her piercing looks and comments.

"*Bahu*, haven't your parents ever taught you how to make halva?" or "When will you learn how to look after your elders – everything you are doing is for yourself."

I felt like grabbing her neck and throttling life out of her, but I kept quiet for Amarjit's sake. Despite her pointed utterances, he was very loyal to her, obedient and demure all through her stay. I heaved a big sigh of relief when she went to Canada, still moaning and grumbling about everything she had come across in England.

Life with Amarjit was busy, but I had no serious complaints and the care that I got from him was very touching. My marriage was like a still lake, without any ripples or tides. There wasn't much excitement that could make my heart beat faster but, at the same time, there was not anything that could make me pine for some other life. I had three children, two boys and a girl. The boys, Raj and Dev, went to the local state school and consistently got positive comments from their teachers. My daughter, Hina, was very close to me and turned out to be a high achiever at school. I was content with my life, so the ancient flame burning in my heart for further education got slowly extinguished as I got busy with bringing up my children and improving the quality of my home.

Amarjit, too, was content with his life and the lack of any hobbies to engage him did not cause him any stress. He spent a lot of his free time working in the garden and was increasingly proud of the range of shrubs and flowering plants which had transformed the entire view at the rear of the house. We had Amarjit's brothers and sister regularly turning the emotional screw to get some money sent to them, but even that did not cause us any loss of sleep. We revelled in looking after our family and felt pleasure in making sacrifices for our children.

There used to be at times though a half-forgotten craving for further studies in my mind. While in India, I used to dream about being a writer of novels and short stories in Punjabi. I was a voracious reader of Puran Singh, Jaswant Singh Kanwal, Sant Singh Sekhon, Amrita Pritam and a whole lot of other well-known Punjabi authors. But now the embers of my ambition were hardly smouldering, however, buried under the day-to-day seldom-changing chores of running a household.

The house wasn't very hospitable to books as Amarjit would only read the evening newspaper or occasionally *The Sunday Times*. All his time was spent on his job or out in the garden. It was obvious that he was very much in his element only when looking after his house, children and garden. I was, on the other hand, sometimes feeling disconsolate at being unable to go beyond household chores and looking after my family. In order to have a break from the monotony of daily life, I developed an interest in retail therapy, browsing in different shops in Dudley and looking out for discounted clothes or things that could enhance the décor at home.

Also, I had a circle of close friends and we used to meet up from time to time. They were from similar backgrounds in India and had come to England after marriage. They, too, worked in factories, living in extended families, every now and then, desperately seeking relief from the daily grind. They shared their family tribulations in confidence over a cup of tea and digestives. We used to spend hours doing just that.

I was close to Sumeera, who was rather stout, but had endearing traits, with a penchant for talking, sharing the news about her extended family and sometimes griping about her insouciant husband who, though caring, was given to sudden changes in mood. She worked part-time and whenever she could snatch a moment or two, she would frequent local stores or even stores in nearby towns to pass her time looking for bargains. We used to have good gossiping sessions, punctuated by laughter, occasionally tears and eating copious amount of pizza and homemade sweet concoctions. I felt it was, in a way, not very different from the microcosm of society in Rawal Pindi that my mum had experienced all those decades ago.

7

After six years, we moved to a cul-de-sac about a mile from our old house. It was considered to be an upmarket area at that time as the houses were spacious with good-sized gardens.

The whole street was bathed in serenity and calm. No traffic or noise reverberated through the pavements outside these houses and gardens looked meticulously manicured. The residents of the street seemed very cultured, being reserved, but helpful at the same time and obviously had a sense of civic pride in their environment. It took us about two years to get to know most of the neighbours who, to our delight, were welcoming and willing to help us settle into our new home. Over time, the street underwent big changes in its population and there was a consequent impact on the quality of life there.

I got involved in many neighbourly activities and shared joys and sorrows with many of the residents.

George, my next-door neighbour, was a stoical person

with a spartan lifestyle. He had lost his wife more than ten years ago and lived on his own, seldom venturing out of the house, except for shopping or getting his monthly haircut. He liked his own company and, despite his reticence, was a caring person. He was very traditional in his outlook and only Black Country food was allowed in his ancient fridge-freezer. To him, aubergines, peppers or even courgettes were exotic vegetables. Instead, black pudding, faggots, grey peas and pork scratchings used to inspire his taste buds. Whenever he was ill, I would go in and do his shopping for him. He insisted on paying and always brought out a jar full of silver and copper coins to give me. I admired his determination to live and not let any frailties or occasional bouts of illness deter him from his daily routine.

Decades later, when he died, he left all his assets to Ann, his wife's niece, who, as soon as she got the money in her account after the sale of his house, dumped her husband and went to have a holiday in the Caribbean. Mike, her husband, remained unfazed at this unforeseen turn of events and even revelled in his newfound life as a bachelor. Within a year, he found another partner as I discovered when I bumped into him in Tipton's High Street where he was strutting about with his arm around his new woman's waist.

Another neighbour, Ian, was a rather inelegantly dressed man with deep furrows and crevices on every bit of his face. I was struck by the huge change that had overtaken him since his father's death. Guy, his father, used to be a very well-dressed, pukka Englishman with impeccable manners. Depression, or a gnawing sense of loneliness, perhaps, impacted Ian very badly and he morphed into a strange incarnation. He had been living with his parents and, after his loss, Ian became a recluse and neglected his appearance and health.

He had repeated bouts of illness and was in the grip of a fear that made him spend much of his time indoors. He had four cars on his drive, all old and which spluttered and coughed rabidly when coaxed to start, and a number of cats. I used to see him sometimes out in his front garden as dusk was descending. I could see him holding an old camera and taking pictures of his cars from different angles. His cats were lovely, well-fed and always playful. But the occasional wailing noise they made in the middle of the night was very disconcerting.

Ian lived under the delusion that he had a talent for musical composition and would one day get a call from Hollywood. His salvation, though it was only a part-salvation admittedly, came when he started to spend time with Barbara, another neighbour who was a widow in her sixties. If you wanted to learn how not to look, you did not need to go very far.

She had fine-tuned her bedraggled looks and made it her mission to wear only out-of-fashion second-hand clothes, probably from a charity shop. She had mastered the art of hobbling along with her back slightly bent like someone carrying the heavy burden of age. They were happy though and spent most of their time toing and froing from one house to the other. I think that was the only exercise they were getting, walking that distance of twenty or so metres between their houses about fifteen times every day. However, they would always come out to say hello to me if ever I went into the front garden. I used to like the apologetic, self-effacing tone of Ian's voice when asking about our well-being.

Gary lived in the bungalow at the end of the cul-de-sac with his mother, Pat. Pat was physically unable to go out of the bungalow without assistance. Her husband had been the head teacher of a primary school in Bridgenorth, but died prematurely long before his retirement. Hodgson's Lymphoma caught him unawares, as cancer always does, and after an initial round of chemotherapy, he died a painful death in a hospice.

Gary was a gentleman whose life had been scarred by Crohn's disease and it had cost him his job and self-confidence. He loved doing little jobs for his neighbours though and spent his time looking after his mother. He was a much-loved character in the immediate neighbourhood and had a little stock of well-worn jokes. We heard the same jokes, the same turns of phrase time and time again and we could see him deriving a huge amount of enjoyment from regurgitating them. A chat with Gary was always welcomed by the residents of our street. He was a friendly person with a mischievous, but gentle, much-trodden sense of humour. He didn't survive for many years though, and, one stormy night, he died in his sleep.

Jag and his wife, Pammi, also lived in the same street with their four children. They moved into their home when the previous owners, Stephen and Lisa, moved to Wales after retirement. Jag had come over to England from Punjab and found the life in this country a paradise.

In India, he didn't have a job and had no burning desire for studies. Fortunately for him, he had found an agent who could arrange his journey to this country. He mortgaged the little land that he had inherited from his parents and arrived here and went to the local college and became a clerk in the office of a foundry in Tipton.

Jag had no other interest than amassing money. After his stint in the foundry office, he found work in a building society as a cashier, plus he also had a couple of houses rented out and he enjoyed counting his financial assets every night. His wife, Pammi, was a baptised Sikh and both of them had a tape recorder for playing Sikh devotional songs throughout the day.

They were, however, good neighbours, always willing and ready to help others in the street.

Jag thought he was endowed with the finest skills to tackle any job around the house, so his grandstanding advice, usually unsolicited, could be very boring at times.

He had two hobbies apart from saving: washing his and other family cars and gardening. His garden was pristine, with a manicured lawn having razor-sharp edges and a cornucopia of shrubs and flowers. Most of the shrubs migrated to his garden as saplings he had scrounged from his relatives and friends. He did not believe in spending money. He was an uncle to most of the residents in the street as he did not need persuasion to dispense his advice on any issue raised in the course of an ordinary conversation. He kept himself updated on the latest happenings on the estate and shared them with everyone in the street.

Days and night in that neighbourhood were spent without any seismic events. Amarjit and I lived a life without any tidal events. I applied myself to looking after the house and, in my spare time, browsed in shops looking for bargains at sales. Their voracious appetite for presents kept me busy stocking garments, shoes and bottles of perfume for future visits to my home village. Over time, I had something akin to an addiction to going to sales and rummaging through discounted wares with an eye on the future needs of the extended family.

What used to fill me with a slight sense of disgust was when those relatives used to scrutinise the gifts we had taken for them and ask questions like, "Are they from Marks and Spencer's? We don't wear clothes bought from other shops." I used to look at their shabby clothes, with several islands of dirt clinging to them after having returned from their fields and simultaneously laughed and cried in my mind.

We found matches for our boys and they got married and went to their respective jobs in Leicester and Manchester. Hina moved out of the house and purchased a terraced house and got an opportunity to contribute to a couple of newspapers. Eventually, Hina found a partner of her own choice. We soon warmed to Steve as both of them began visiting us in Dudley on a regular basis. Steve worked in the sales and promotions department of a glossy local magazine and was invariably polite and respectful in our dealings with him and very caring with our daughter.

The tumultuous period of married life when you are busy looking after your young children and gathering paraphernalia to enhance your home was coming to an end.

I always dreaded going to India with Amarjit because I had to spend months garnering presents for his undeserving relatives. I used to go over to Bangalore spend a few days with my brothers' families to escape from the drudgery of waiting for a smile from Amarjit's siblings and their families.

Amarjit's late brother, Gian, still had his family living in the ancestral village. His daughter-in-law, Preeti, looked quite daunting. She had the build of a wrestler, a tongue that could spew a torrent of words, punctuated by juicy expletives, and an appetite that only a horse could only dream of. Her husband, Jasbir, was living under a severe delusion that his wife was the epitome of femininity, endowed with unsurpassed beauty.

She had grandiose dreams of becoming a Bollywood actress with hordes of people following her, waiting for her autograph. Preeti did not like to do any household chores and had no interest in cooking. She had an old maid called Jaswinder, who did all the cooking in a makeshift kitchen out in the open.

Jasbir was even more timid than an ailing mouse in her presence and had come to terms with her claim that she was not born to do any manual work. She terrorised her neighbours as she could curse and deploy a vast range of expletives in her sonorous voice. On our visits, when we unpacked our suitcases, she used to take the first choice of any clothes for herself and if Amarjit's sister, Jeeto, was there from Nakuru, both of them were like eagles homing in on the best morsels.

Although not clearly articulated, I knew that Amarjit would find happiness if he set up a home for retirement in India. Many of the immigrants from his part of the Punjab had done the same. They had used their savings to build *kotthis* or little mansions in their ancestral village and they found reverting to their childhood very comforting. Some of them made such a move in their sixties and there were a few cases when some them set up home there in their seventies. Amarjit was often nostalgic about the time he had spent in India and, in support of his statements, would allude to happenings that occurred in his childhood and young adulthood in his village over half a century ago.

I felt very differently. England, to me, was a country where I had considerable freedom and independence. I could buy things for myself and choose what food I wanted to eat without any direction from males in the family. Even when I was waiting to get married, I did not have the kind of freedom I had in England. In India, I had to look for acceptance and approval from my parents or brothers. But, here, I was the architect of my own destiny. I knew from the very outset that my adopted country was going to be my permanent home. I often remarked to my English colleagues at work, I could go back to India regularly with anticipation of joy and excitement, but only for a few weeks at a time.

The sense of ennui that I used to experience during those visits was often overwhelming. Most of the villagers who had gone abroad used to spend all their vacation time sitting on a string bed by the tube well of their farms and not venture out to explore any other parts of India. Their concept of a holiday was to spend as much time as possible with relatives from their parental families.

Most of the young people in the village had turned themselves into drug addicts. There was a deluge of narcotics available with the blessing of the police and politicians. Poppies, opium, ganja, heroin, white or brown powder, spice – there was a big choice being peddled on the street every day. Most of the young men, often dying to have a hit, would congregate and wait for the drug dealer or their representative to arrive so that they could have their fix for the day. Gian's two sons – the younger one still under sixteen – would spend their day in a stupor, lying in a room, barely conscious, oblivious to their surroundings. Once the effect of the drug began to wane, they would wake up from their defunctive slumber to have another fix.

8

Life was being lived without too many high points or landmarks to ignite nostalgia in my maturing years. The inevitable monotony of cleaning the house, feeding the family, food shopping, providing children with homemade food on their regular visits, bargain-hunting in shops to satisfy the insatiable greed of relatives in India – all my time after work was laid at the altar of family life. I forgot how to have an occasional treat or pamper myself. I wasn't exactly experiencing effervescent joy, but, nevertheless, feeling happy in a calm, altruistic way. I was doing my duty towards my family; it gave me no cause for disquietude.

I had got used to living the life I was living. I had come to terms with the sameness. I found myself seeking comfort in my daily chores and routines. The fact that the house was clean and tidy and there was a willingness and resources at hand to offer hospitality to visitors and the fact that my children were doing well, carving out careers for themselves, were the things that I found consoling. The reading of love poetry by Amrita Pritam or Shiv Batalvi occasionally reminded me of another universe that had become alien to me, but was soon forgotten in the day-to-day repetitive jobs around the house. Also, I found a job in a dry-cleaning shop and that kept me occupied, leaving little room for daydreaming.

The dry-cleaning shop, owned by an English man called Arthur, was in Sedgley, a town only a mile away from Dudley. I had a reasonable grasp of English and was able to sustain simple conversation with customers. The work did not make any heavy demands on me and I was able to function effectively without any excessive stress. In order to fill the time in between the customers bringing their washing or dry cleaning, I used to tune into the radio and listen to pop. Though very different from the Punjabi songs of my childhood, these were, nonetheless, very calming to the ears. I was able to recall many melodious tunes in moments of solitude, though I was not always able to understand the lyrics.

Six months into my job there, I grew familiar and felt at home with the tasks entrusted to me.

One day, Arthur asked me to move to his second shop, which was much closer to where we lived. No commuting was involved and I could walk to the shop from home within ten minutes. I mentioned it to the next customer who came into the shop with his washing and he casually said, "Love, we'll miss you!"

I thought he really meant that and burst out crying. The same thing happened when another loyal customer responded, "Good luck! We'll miss you!"

Again, the floodgates of tears opened wide and I thought I was taking a leap in the dark by deserting all my customers who really, really had affection for me! It was years later that I realised I had forgotten to read between the lines and mistaken mere pleasantries for solemn statements of appreciation.

The glimpses into another life that I snatched from conversations with Anita sometimes made me wonder if I was missing out on something.

Anita was a colleague in the new Dudley shop. She was married with two children and had a very different lifestyle. Going out at weekends, eating at restaurants and going to the cinema and on holidays which definitely did not involve visiting relatives. Her prioritisation of personal enjoyment and finding time for herself haunted my mind late at night and, at times, kept me awake. Her husband, Ian, showed her a lot of affection and she told me about celebrating Valentine's Day or their wedding anniversary and birthdays. These things were completely alien to me. The most I got was a greeting card on my birthday, without any subsequent celebrations, except perhaps an Indian pudding with the evening meal.

Anita and Ian used to go to warmer countries for their holidays and most of the places she spoke about were on a different planet for me. However, it was only the occasional stray thought that I found troubling. Most of the time, I was content because it was all nothing short of a fairy tale to me. And, when I thought of some of my acquaintances and the miserable life they had to experience, I was grateful for what I had got.

Manjit, one of my neighbours, had her life made hell by some of her husband's relatives who also lived nearby. She was her husband's second wife after the sudden departure of his first wife on grounds of incompatibility. She was constantly being treated very harshly or called abusive names such as," whore", "housebreaker" and "the witch haunting our family" by members of his extended family who thought she had a hand in breaking up her husband's first marriage.

She spent all her time sewing or mending clothes and her lounge was full of bits of fabric, as well as ready or yet to be readied garments, along with a couple of sewing machines. She used to visit me occasionally to shed a tear or two over what she used to term her destiny.

Her husband, a nice man with the professional training to be an accountant, would listen to her complain about the appalling behaviour of his siblings and their families, but he always chose to remain silent. He didn't have the courage to defend her and merely tried to console her that things would get better in the future. Eventually, they moved to another part of the town, away from those monstrous relatives. She seemed to be more content in her new setting, but, from time to time, the ghosts of her troubled experiences continued to haunt her. She found it difficult to trust any relatives after her move.

I did not have any unsavoury issues to contend with. Amarjit was caring, bought food for the family and gave me considerable freedom to go out shopping. He was supportive of my plans to enhance the house after his customary initial reluctance and was always ready to spend money on projects to make our home a better place to live in.

At work, I had part of a tightly knit group of women and we used to meet up from time to time at each other's homes to talk, consigning the mundane worries of running households to the litter bin of memory and generally have a good time eating, drinking tea, laughing and gossiping. The friendship bonds which had firmed up over years helped me overcome any troubling thoughts of isolation and their company somehow compensated for the loss of the Eden that I once had in mind while a young girl in India.

I was constantly reminded of the fragility of arranged marriages whenever I saw newly married brides trying to come to terms with being in a strange home in a strange country.

Opposite our house lived Ram Lal, my husband's contemporary, who worked as a bus conductor in Dudley and knew Amarjit very well. His younger brother, Tony, was persuaded or even perhaps told to import a bride from India. I warmed up to Ritu, his bride, and found her very sophisticated in her manners, polite, but a little too docile and timid. She was very comely with defined attractive features.

Ram Lal and his wife, Kamla, somehow did not make any effort to welcome her into their joint family and started to be hypercritical of anything she tried to do. If she was tasked to do the washing up after meals, Kamla lost no opportunity to point out to Ritu that the dishes were not spotless. If she cleaned the carpet in the drawing room with a soft brush as they did not have a vacuum cleaner, she would point to the specks of fluff or strands of fibre or other miniscule detritus still waiting to be removed.

I was not aware that Kamla wanted Ritu to marry her niece who was still in India. Ram Lal was a silent partner in this ongoing one-sided feud and did not think it was his place to intervene as Kamla filled Ritu's life with unmitigated misery and, at the same time, turned Tony against her.

I noticed the sudden change in Tony's attitude towards his wife whom he idolised at his wedding. I could see a warm glow on his face when the newly-wedded couple used our garden ideal for capturing their joy in a post-wedding photo shoot. But now Tony was trying to keep his distance, his face dyed with a permanent gloom. The drastic change that I noticed within six months of their wedding was unhinging for me.

When I saw Ritu being pushed into a cab to take her to Heathrow to fly her back to India, I was deeply disturbed. I could imagine how Ritu's parents must have felt when they saw their daughter come back under such a dark cloud. Tongues must have wagged in their home town. I was sure the people there must have judged Ritu guilty and believed she must have done something heinous to warrant expulsion from her husband's family. The sense of mortification and humiliation her parents experienced would surely have left them broken.

Amarjit was very caring and mindful of my need for reassurance, but, at the same time, he was very close to his parental family.

Amarjit could not desist from sending money to his brothers and sister in India whose appetite for free wads of rupees was insatiable. However, the slights dished out by his mother or the tantrums displayed by his sister did not cause any tremors in my mind because Amarjit was steadfast in his care and respect for me. I had learnt how to bury my emotions and apply myself to being a committed wife and mother. I lived and breathed my family and did everything I possibly could to contribute to its well-being. Education beyond school had eluded me and I was determined that my children would get my blood, sweat and tears to help them realise their dreams concerning building careers for themselves after university.

After our children's weddings were over, a burden had lifted off our shoulders and we thought we would be able to enjoy our freedom as we advanced towards the late afternoon of our life. I had done my duty, I thought, by giving as much support as possible to my children to do well in higher education, helping them find their partners and paying for their elaborate weddings. Now was the time to relax, take life in our stride and enjoy the rest of our precious time on this planet.

One day when I was at a loose end, I went to the Churchill Shopping Centre which had lost many of its well-known stores and was now a collection of small units and closed shutters. I walked into Asda to pass the time, expecting not to purchase anything and I saw a figure choosing a wine bottle after a good spell of concentration. As he turned around with a bottle of red wine in his hand, his face looked familiar. I didn't take long for me to realise that he was Shivraj whom I had briefly met in Sidhwan just minutes before I'd gone in to attend a lecture. My heart skipped a beat and my face instantly felt red. It did not take Shivraj long, too, to recall that fateful encounter.

We came out of the store and, over a cup of coffee, went over the huge chasm of time that had separated us. After filling each other in on what had happened in our lives, we promised to meet up again, my head still spinning about, how of all the places in the world, he happened to be in Dudley where I had settled more than twenty-five years ago.

Our conversation was nothing more than going over the milestones of our life, such as our emigration, marriage, children and other mundane happenings. But the shooting stars in my heart continued to fly. I was slightly drunk thinking about what might have been if fate had not intervened to separate us so abruptly and if I had had the slightest courage to respond to him in that tiny village in Punjab all those years ago.

The heavy weight of the past and the expectations of our present family responsibilities kept our interaction at a very pleasant, but an entirely unexciting level. Our families got closer to each other and meeting on social occasions became more and more frequent.

Shivraj, who was a probation officer in the neighbouring

town of Stourbridge, gave us invaluable advice on many occasions and we hugely valued his experience and knowledge of the British mores. We used to look forward to his visits. My tenderness towards him remained subterranean, however, and resurfaced only through my welcoming hospitality.

During one of her many visits to our house, Dalbir once mentioned in sobbing tones how her son, Ranjit, had distanced himself from his wife, Kirti. Dalbir was very fond of Kirti. She liked her company and both of them enjoyed doing things together. Kirti was still doing all the cooking and cleaning in their house and Dalbir regularly took her to the *gurdwara* and the local shopping centre. Dalbir had a bubbly, foaming personality and enjoyed the simple pleasures of life. When she was depressed in the slightest, the same degree of over-reaction enveloped her body and mind.

Visits to the local Pizza Hut used to provide her with an enormous amount of lift and Kirti used to silently revel in feasting on pizza with her mother-in-law who, despite taking the side of Ranjit on several occasions, still showed care towards her.

Dalbir's cousin, Balbir, was also a frequent visitor at our house. She, too, had mentioned Kirti's plight to me. No one, however, was willing or able to pinpoint the exact reason for Ranjit's drifting apart from Kirti. My heart used to melt whenever I listened to Dalbir's agonising story about the turn of events in her family. Kirti was doubly related to Dalbir, as she was the daughter of her brother's wife who lived in Uganda. She had to tread on eggshells and be mindful of the hurt her son's sorry saga could cause to a number of people in her extended family.

Here was this girl from a village – simple, innocent, unaware of the dangers lurking out there in society. She had been uprooted from her village and brought to a strange country, which was an entirely new world to her. She did not have any skills or qualifications that could provide her with security or independence. Ranjit, the man chosen to be her husband, was free to do anything he liked, wallowing in self-indulgence, drinking and wasting time in the company of a motley crowd of drinking buddies. There was nothing she could do to instil commonsense into his head. I wanted to support her.

Almost a year passed before I learned, again from Balbir, that Ranjit was living with Samantha, who lived only a short distance from their house in the very next street. It was difficult to imagine anyone more uninviting than Samantha, an obese woman about ten years older than Ranjit with an insatiable appetite for pies and pasties. She already had four children from her previous marriage to Jeffery whom she had kicked out of her council house because of his addiction to drugs. Kirti was slim, clean-looking and bashful, whereas Samantha was loud, garish and rather uncouth in her manners. What did Ranjit see in her?

Dalbir didn't mention Ranjit's decamping to Samantha's house, but I got it from Balbir and I was in a state of shock for several days. Since I thought it was Dalbir who should be breaking the news about Ranjit's infidelity to Kirti, I kept it to myself, but I began inviting Kirti to my house more often. I used to treat her like a daughter, giving her little presents and surrounding her with warmth and affection.

Ranjit, during one of his visits to his parents' house, thrust a sheaf of papers into Kirti's hands and asked her to sign them. He had decided to divorce her on grounds of incompatibility. Kirti signed the papers and spent the next fortnight silently crying within her claustrophobic room.

Without mentioning any details of her case, I asked all my friends to start looking for a suitable man for her to marry. After a lot of toing and froing, I managed to find a newly-arrived immigrant to this country, who was more than willing to marry her. Within a couple of months, they got married and despite the constant precautions that Gurdial, the new man in Kirti's life, had to undertake, they seemed to have found some happiness together in their rented apartment. The hurt that Kirti had felt never went away though and, on her occasional visits to my house, her eyes would often moisten.

Looking back at the emotions that Kirti's plight provoked in me, I can see now that my sense of outrage and urgency to support her was focused on the appalling situation that had been thrust upon her.

In my personal life at home, I tried to stand up for my rights, though I had to argue my case sensitively at times. Apart from the initial resistance that I inevitably encountered, Amarjit, most of the time, heard what I would say and accepted my reasoning for demanding an equal say in family matters.

Kirti got swallowed up in the daily chores of running her new home and gradually we drifted apart. Dalbir was relieved when Kirti moved out of her room and settled in with Gurdial. Within a few months, Ranjit declared that he was going to make his union with Samantha official. Although Dalbir had lost some of her fizziness that she originally felt when Kirti joined her family, she took the new developments in her stride and the wedding ceremony of her son and his partner was solemnised in Willenhall.

Samantha did not want to have frequent contact with Ranjit's family and was very territorial when visiting or entertaining his relatives. She had the gift of the gab, but it seemed to Dalbir that, most of the time, Samantha was speaking without any context or relevance to her. During their meet-ups, which tapered off within a few months, Ranjit was often the silent spectator, watching Samantha wide-eyed with adulation. The gulf between Ranjit, Samantha and Dalbir's family grew wider and wider until their visits marked only certain key events, such as Christmas or a few family birthdays.

9

One morning, Amarjit complained that he had developed a nagging backache, not an ordinary backache, but something more ferocious that kept him awake at night. He had experienced a slipped disc a decade ago and we thought there was maybe a resurgence of pain from the same area. After some physical exertion, he needed to lie down to let the backache recede a little. He went to the GP's surgery, but returned home with only a tube of Deep Relief to rub into his back. He began to suffer backache more often, but chose to do so in silence, persisting to massage in the Deep Relief and soothing his pain with hot water bottles or ibuprofen.

The pain did not pester him all the time, so Amarjit carried on working part-time, although he had reached retirement age a few years ago. He did not want to degenerate due to not having a purpose. He was, in a way, a bit concerned about what he would do to fill his vacant hours if he were to retire completely.

The GP was contacted again and Amarjit was given stronger painkillers which worked for a short while, but his body got accustomed to them and began to cry for something more potent to assuage the stinging misery afflicting his back.

Steroid injections were the next course of treatment. They worked for a bit, but the pain returned with a vengeance. Perhaps he needed a decent break from the work that he had been doing continuously throughout decades of his life. We decided to go to his village in India for a couple of weeks. The tranquillity of the village and the stillness of life there might make him feel better, we thought.

The break in his ancestral village did not do anything to temper his suffering. The members of his extended family were obviously more concerned with extracting more and more money from him than doing anything practical to make him feel better. As his pain began to increase exponentially, Amarjit was feeling more and more disenchanted about the conspicuous lack of familial support. He had helped members of his extended family financially on numerous occasions, but his folks there showed complete indifference to his deteriorating health.

We still put his persistent back pain down to his hard work over the years and blamed his job. Amarjit, however, remained stoical and did not complain too often and attributed it to the travails of being an immigrant in a foreign country.

On returning from India, he went back to his GP again

and was given another steroid injection. Much of our time was spent waiting for the injections to take effect. Eventually, after aeons of putting up with pain, his GP referred him to the hospital for a blood test. The blood test took place at the Dudley Guest Hospital. An agonising wait in the assessment unit there saw him writhing in pain, going without food for hours with uncertainties plaguing his consciousness. He felt alone and so did the whole family as we sat there.

Around midnight, we left him, still waiting for a doctor to be free to investigate the source of pain radiating from his back. The blood and other diagnostic tests took eight hours and were completed by the early hours of the morning. I felt completely helpless, sitting at home waiting for his return.

The very next day we got a call from the hospital asking us to go and see a consultant about the blood test results. I knew it was going to be bad news. This made me panic, which I tried to keep shut out from the ever-closing in walls of my whole being. When the consultant said that Amarjit was suffering from advanced Hodgkinson Lymphoma, neither of us could register the gravity of the news.

I gathered that it was a kind of cancer, but I somehow felt it was a cancer that was curable and would be treated successfully. Amarjit was still upbeat, chiefly because he did not fully understand the bomb that had exploded in that consultant's room.

When we were driving back home from the hospital, he turned towards me and said, exuding some subdued confidence,

"I am going to defeat this disease. I know I am going to live up to the age of ninety."

Although the consultant did his best to explain how that particular kind of cancer impacted on the survival of patients and the various options of treatment available at the hospital, I had not been able to take anything in, except a realisation that this was something very serious. I could not think anything beyond that. Our priority was to get the treatment regime going as soon as possible.

During the journey home, I did not say much. I merely held his hand in the vain hope that he would find that reassuring.

As soon as we returned home, I rang my children and then I asked Shivraj to look on the internet about the nature of this unknown beast which was pounding hard on our door.

After that fateful encounter in Asda, Shivraj had been our family friend for over three decades. He was now a manager in the probation service in the Black Country. He was a well-read person, with a very polite, courteous demeanour. We used to meet up socially three or four times a year and sometimes he and his wife, Puneet, used to spend a couple of hours with us. We used to look forward to welcoming them on such visits and took great care to offer them snacks and a drink. I did not find it easy to look at his glowing face and often spoke with him without looking him in the eye.

I was, however, certain that he, too, liked to come to our house.

As time went on, our paths diverged, however, as Shivraj

got busy with furthering his career and I spent all my time supporting my children to achieve as much academic success as they possibly could.

In the middle of my son Dev's A' level examinations, I had a telephone call from India to say that my mother had died in India where she was staying with my brother, Hardev, and his family. Just a few days before Dev's examinations had begun, while on way to work, but still close to our house, I had been wondering how long she was going to survive without my father who, just a few years earlier, had succumbed to another massive stroke.

I told Amarjit about the devastating news from India, how my mum, too, had suffered a stroke which had left her paralysed, unable to move or do anything. Both Amarjit and I decided not to mention this tragic news to Dev so as not to disrupt his revision schedule. Amarjit and I spent the entire night sitting, weeping silently, but hiding our grief. Dev sat his examinations and got some decent grades and went to Hull University.

Years passed and now, when approaching retirement, I was trying very hard to grapple with Amarjit's backache. In order to prove his tenacity and determination, he would work in the garden for a couple of hours and then collapse in utter exhaustion.

Shivraj turned out to be great support to both of us and provided timely and much-needed support during my husband's debilitating chemotherapy and numerous blood transfusions. Shivraj had more freedom as he was nearing his retirement and his job gave him more flexibility to manage his own time.

Actually, we got closer to Shivraj much earlier than that when his wife was snatched away from him by a sudden ambush by cancer. She was relatively young, in the prime of her life, and both of them had an idyllic married life together.

Her illness was discovered during a routine check-up at the local hospital and the rapid decline in her health took everyone by surprise. I was so moved by Shivraj's pain that I wrote many poems to express my shock and sympathy. Amarjit and I began to visit his house regularly to lend an ear to his outpouring of grief. We also took food to him from time to time and did our bit to help with his household chores. The intensity of pain in his eyes and the depth of his despair at losing his partner took over my thoughts and I resolved to provide him continuing, albeit mostly silent, support.

Amarjit did not seem to have the lexicon or confidence to offer his condolences, whereas I was able to offer my shared pain through my poems and questions about his well-being. Our encounters became more and more regular and we felt we had a duty to offer help and assistance to Shivraj in his hour of need.

10

8th September

A sense of loneliness, searing and unfathomable, whenever I come home after work in the evening, overpowers my whole being and I cannot help howling in the emptiness that engulfs me. Reining in my emotions no longer remains within my reach and a surge of dark, melancholy thoughts flood my mind. All I can think of are Puneet's final moments, submerged in sheer hopelessness, when she knew that she had entered the last stage of her life. Both of us knew that an ocean of nothingness lay ahead, pulling her into its bottomless abyss.

I couldn't seek solace in the recall of occasions in our married life which used to make me inebriated with joy. Perhaps all that happened in another life. I could not forget Puneet's face while the dusk was being hijacked by an unforgiving blackness.

"Where have you gone?" was the question that haunted me. In her final days, Puneet said to me on a number of occasions, "Shivraj, you must learn to live on your own. I won't be around for long. Please learn how to cope without me."

Those brief conversations, when dusk was preparing to decimate the entire view out of our window, were painful. At times, it seemed only a dream. Only a dream and nothing more than that.

28th November

The nightmare proved to be true though and Puneet left me for ever. In stunned disbelief, I could not fully comprehend the enormity of my loss. The arrangements around her funeral did not leave much time for any real mourning. I was like a robot, carrying out tasks to make sure her departure was marked appropriately. Grief was tightening its grip around my neck and all I could see ahead of me was darkness – the unmitigated, absolute darkness of despair, desolation and infinite emptiness.

6th December

My ruptured heart showed no signs of healing as the darkness in my soul grew deeper as time went on and left me little time to think of anything else, but the last few days and moments of togetherness with Puneet. I did not have the ability to recall the happier, slightly inebriated, times that Puneet and I had frequently enjoyed together. All I could think of was her final moments, the agony of uncertainty that she must have gone through before leaving me lost and disorientated in a world that was, in her absence, unfamiliar to me. She was fully cognisant of the immediacy of the ending of her existence on this earth. The shadow of her final moments bore heavily on my memory and left me on the verge of a mental collapse.

All those who felt even the slightest sympathy for the misery in which my whole body and soul was sinking tried to console me with the age-old adage that time is a great healer. Time, however, had thrust me into a maelstrom of doubts as to whether there was anything else that I could have done to save the love of my life. I detected a strident sense of guilt buried deep in my mind. Everything I did, everything I touched and every thought that entered my head reminded me of what I had lost forever. I began to lose interest in almost everything that once used to engage me. The daily chores and routines seemed superfluous and irrelevant with Puneet no longer around me.

Maninder's visits and conversations were, however, the only thing I began to look forward to. The dialogue with her was one-sided, me doing all the talking, reminiscing, lamenting, crying and she listening to me patiently. All this was very cathartic.

I found myself waiting for our next get-together so that I could again drown myself in the unbridgeable chasm of separation that had emerged after Puneet's death. I found Maninder's presence consoling, as if she was gradually trying to drink in my grief. Apart from the material comforts that she brought with her, such as food, these conversations with her made me feel wanted, slowly dragging me out of depression. With hindsight, I could feel that my grief had found a voice in her sympathetic company.

16ᵗʰ October

I spent a little bit of time at Maninder's house and, as I was leaving, she stood on her drive and said, "Look, there is a full moon in the sky. It looks pure magic, spellbinding, more magnificent and divine than anything else on earth."

I stood enthralled, gazing briefly at the moon and then at Maninder's face. I had a sudden urge to "fan the moonbeams from her face". A silent murmur echoed in my head:

What counsel has the hooded moon
Put in thy heart, my shyly sweet
Of love in ancient plenitude...

My mind was like a dervish, revelling in the poetry inspired by the moon in Urdu and English. W.H. Davies' poem, Moon, swept through my mind and my dancing heart was echoing his words:

Though there are birds that sing this night
With thy white beams across their throats
Let my deep silence speak for me
More than for them their sweetest notes...

I stood gazing at the moon. Its celestial light was so bright that we could even see, with surprising detail, the contours of its mountains. I thought of many poetic allusions to damsels and reticent girls with their hearts bursting with love and desire, but being unable to articulate anything about it in simple words, I came back home. I picked up the phone when I got home and blurted out: "Maninder, I think I am falling in love with you."

I was astonished to hear myself utter those words – where did it all come from? After a brief discussion, Maninder, to my sheer relief, returned my sentiments.

As I put the phone down, I knew that I had crossed the Rubicon. My future was going to change completely and irrevocably. This new development in my life was not going to morph my grief into anything different, but there was inevitably going to be a new dimension to my thinking and future. She might have alluded to the beauty of a full moon in a matter-of-fact way without any subtext. My inference that she was impelled by tender feelings was perhaps rooted in the numerous poems about the pull of moonlight for lovers in romantic poetry.

10th November

Finding someone to listen to you, to hear when you are screaming within, in your sixties, is something very rare in Punjabi or any other culture. Widowhood is considered to be the signal for retreat from normal life, withdrawing into your own unforgiving world of loneliness. Your families, relatives and friends might throw morsels of consoling words now and then, but your daily life is untouched by real sympathy or even understanding. You are really the bottom of the heap, discarded, left to your own devices, while those who are allegedly close to you carry on with their own lives.

Maninder was the only person who cried when I cried, who did things day in and day out while I was mourning. And her generous support was totally unselfish, expecting nothing in return. I found her company very reassuring. But she was still married to Amarjit and I did not want to cast a shadow over that relationship. Every bit of support that Maninder gave me had to be meticulously planned beforehand or given furtively. Our meetings grew more and more frequent and the few hours she spent with me while Amarjit was busy at work were calming and comforting.

Maninder rang me, I think for the first time, offering words of sympathy and talking about the need to be strong enough to cope with my grief and offering her support. She alluded to the ephemeral nature of life, how the destiny of humans is grief with only few fleeting interludes of happiness. She recited a couple of verses that she had penned to lessen my pain. I listened to her, but did not have the concentration to completely comprehend what she had read. The seething pain in my mind had blocked out my facility of comprehension.

"Shivraj, you need to talk about Puneet, how you miss her, talk about your pain rather than keep it bottled up," she said to me before finishing the telephone call.

17ᵗʰ December

Maninder and Amarjit came to see me with some food. While I was talking about Puneet, I found it difficult to be coherent or respond to their consoling noises with a suitable response. Amarjit remained quiet and spent much of his time nodding in agreement with his wife, while she did all the talking. Her concern and the sincerity of her words were slightly cathartic. Even a cliché such as, "Shivraj, life is precious, nothing can replace Puneet, but you must look after yourself" sounded comforting, albeit devoid of any real meaning at that moment.

25ᵗʰ December.

Christmas was the worst time of the year for me. While the world was gorging on food and drink and exchanging presents, I was feeling utterly forlorn. Puneet and I used to look forward to having simple routines which used to fill us with anticipation and excitement. Working together in the kitchen to prepare our Christmas meal, contacting our children and siblings to talk about the day, watching television and always setting some time aside for tidying up and reading a book. Whenever we had our children staying with us over the festive season, the house used to be full of noise, laughter and activity. Exchanging presents first thing in the morning while drinking tea used to mean sudden welcome and uplifting surprises. But now the house was empty, I was on my own and had a strong desire for the day to come to an abrupt end so as not to prolong my desolation.

Maninder came to visit me in the late afternoon and brought some Christmas fare which we ate together. I had a glass of wine steeped in memories of Christmases past. I was very grateful for Maninder's company. She stayed only for a couple of hours and had to go back home. Hina had come to spend a couple of days with her mum and dad.

2nd January

New Year came and went. Puneet's untimely departure overshadowed everything that I was doing or thinking and the pain never left me during my waking moments. I was getting more and more disenchanted and disengaged from the world around me, almost willing myself to extinguish my own life. Only Maninder's presence and her preparedness to listen to my rambling memories and make occasional consolatory interjections kept me going. A very slight glimmer of hope shone in the dark recesses of my mind. Perhaps life was worth living, after all, despite the killer blow that Puneet's loss had dealt me. Perhaps the future might see some softening of my piercing pain and, with Maninder's help, I might arrive at the stage when I would feel thankful for the time spent with Puneet, rather than slowly burning at our parting. It was the first time that I felt Maninder could be the catalyst for healing my future.

8ᵗʰ January

While the raging pain in my heart is stubbornly refusing to decrease its intensity, I think I am beginning to find Maninder's company helpful in soothing my internal turmoil. The ache looms large across my mind, but her comforting words do not sound discordant or irrational.

When other friends and relatives counsel acceptance of my destiny, I find it hard to accept worn out clichés or hollow platitudes. They do not understand what it means to lose someone you really love with every breath you take. Maninder's counsel does not ignore the withering pain that I have suffered, but recognises that it is natural to have a haemorrhage of grief from time to time.

26ᵗʰ January

Maninder regularly drives to my house to deliver food and spend some time with me, talking about my well-being. She often recounts her traumatic experiences when she had to deal with the departure of her father and mother from a distance of thousands of miles away. They died in India and since she was not able to provide any practical help in their final hours, her sadness had an overlay of regret. Listening to her and her inability to do anything against the inevitable, somehow, made sense to me, although it did not diminish my pain. The loss of one's parents could be very traumatic, but nothing comes close to the pain of losing one's partner, particularly a partner whose presence fills your lifeblood with the oxygen of hope and dreams.

6th February

I went to Maninder's house straight after work to collect some food for the evening. We got talking about the ephemerality of life and then got distracted by a couple of contemporary political happenings. The Iraqi war, started by Bush and Blair, was claiming hundreds of innocent lives and a suicide bomb blast a couple of days ago outside a police station in Baghdad had killed sixteen people with devastating consequence for their families. More than sixty bystanders were seriously wounded. The incident had been reported in the media almost as an ordinary phenomenon without any thought for the tsunami of fear and deprivation it must have unleashed for those poor families.

"Shivraj, why are there so many divisions in society?" Maninder would often ask me, without expecting a response.

Both of us knew that life had taken a course which we couldn't reverse; we had reached a point of no return.

Two individuals who had known each other for many decades, but without anything else but simple courtesy, respect and sound manners were caught up in a maelstrom of emotions, in a whirlpool of new feelings. This part of the planet was being bathed in the soft light of the moon and Maninder gazing at its ethereal light was the precise moment when I felt I had to let her know how she had nestled into my heart.

14th *February*

I got up at 6 a.m., came downstairs and had a cup of tea with a digestive. As soon as I switched the TV on, I realised it was Valentine's Day. After breakfast, I was expecting Maninder to come as Amarjit was at work. Wasn't today the best time to let Maninder know about my deep affection for her? By the time I had finished my breakfast, I had decided to take Maninder to Warren James jewellers in the Churchill Shopping Centre and buy her a Valentine's present.

She was blissfully unaware of the significance of this special day and I had to go over its mythology and symbolism. She readily agreed to go the jewellers and I bought her a bracelet of 9 carat gold. Was I doing something wrong or even sinful giving a present to a married woman? I had a sense of unease, but the swell of love in my veins persuaded me to come to the conclusion that what we were doing was not wrong, let alone sinful.

18th *March*

A quiet afternoon at home. Amarjit was at work and Maninder had come to see me, looking vibrant in her colourful clothes.

Her face was aglow with excitement, but a bit of residual

shyness added to her appeal. We had tea, scones and lapped up the torrent of warm words emanating from each other. She listened to my tearful reminiscences of my life with Puneet, how incidents, which seemed to be minor and commonplace, were tormenting my soul. I couldn't get Puneet out of my mind and, while I had newly-awakened warmth for Maninder, I spent much of my time recollecting many events that I used to foolishly regard as mundane while Puneet was still with me, but how those very incidents blistered my soul.

4th April

It was the day before I turned sixty. I had lots of dreams about spending my retirement in peace and enjoyment with Puneet.

The toxic racism and covert discrimination that I had encountered when I came over to the UK in the early seventies had dealt a body-blow to my concept of this country, the land of Shakespeare and Keats, the cradle of democracy and fairness. It crushed the image I had carried of its willingness to welcome newcomers and prize merit over colour or ethnicity. The resistance that I had faced filled me with renewed vigour and determination though and I found a niche in my civil service job. I rose through the ranks and became an area manager covering a fairly large swathe of the Black Country. And all this enabled Puneet and me to build, brick by brick, our future.

I was approaching the end of my career, a time to look forward to spending the golden twilight of our lives together and enjoying the fruits of my labour and my constant dedication throughout my working life.

I missed Puneet and surmised about the holiday breaks that we might have enjoyed together. We used to talk about our future plans, prior to her terminal illness, and had made a bucket list of activities that we wanted to undertake before leaving this beautiful planet. The wreckage of these dreams now littered the wilderness of my life.

But now Maninder had rekindled that flame of desire. At least we could spend time together, rather than be swallowed up by loneliness. But it was not going to the same – I was fully aware of the harsh reality staring us in the face. She was still married to Amarjit and there was no reason for their marriage to fall apart. Amarjit was a strong guy from a rural background, muscular, and with a concomitant macho outlook on life. Despite spending several decades in the UK, he still retained the simplistic approach to life, without any deep scrutiny of the big issues in modern life. He was a man of action whose sole purpose in life was to work, earn, save, help relatives in India and live a simple life, never forgetting to take care of his immediate family. He would lose himself in listening to Punjabi songs, reminiscing about his early adulthood in his ancestral village and feeling the glow of warmth towards his early experiences in his farming community in his corner of Punjab.

Our meetings had to be furtive, driven by the excuse of helping each other. And our meetings could not be very regular either.

A lot depended on Amarjit's work rota. There were high walls built around us and it was very difficult to see how those walls could be brought down. The joy of finding each other came with the knowledge that the path ahead was laid with broken shards of glass. Then there was the hostility to such companionship by much of the local Punjabi community. Most of its members had come from rural parts of the state, without much education or sophistication and felt comfortable only in the straightjacket of tradition. Such liaisons in that part of India were not allowed and the usual response was to ostracise the offending accomplices. While things had moved on in India, these traditions had become fossilised in the immigrants' adopted countries. Dudley was the radicalised replica of what Punjab was more than fifty years ago. There was never open hostility shown towards transgressing couples, but all the barbs were targeted behind the scenes, in whispers, in the way they looked at you.

But mutual feelings of love and affection can break all barriers.

21st April

I had a phone call from Maninder about the blood test that Amarjit had taken only a few days before. His backache had started to refuse to ease up, even after resting in bed for hours. The epidural steroid injections were proving to be futile and he was spending more and more of his time immobile. The GP was finally persuaded to arrange for a blood test and, a couple of days after the test, Amarjit was asked to see a consultant at the hospital. It was at that meeting that it was discovered that there were abnormal levels of para-proteins in his blood. A phlebotomist took another sample of blood from a vein in his arm to confirm the diagnosis. At the next appointment, a doctor took a small sample of one of his lymph nodes under his left arm. There was a CT scan taken, too, and a biopsy taken out of his bone marrow. After the battery of tests, it was concluded that Amarjit was suffering from non-Hodgkin Lymphoma.

I accompanied Amarjit and Maninder to the hospital for those tests and was present when the oncologist gave his diagnosis. Amarjit was not visibly upset, although he remained quieter than usual. On return from the hospital, I went onto the internet to see what kind of beast this cancer was and to find out about its prognosis.

24th April

Dr MacManus gave us the prognosis and confirmed that Amarjit had non-Hodgkin Lymphoma, which was relatively indolent or low-grade and developing slowly, but was expected to defy a complete cure.

She delivered the shattering news in a monotone matter-of-fact way. During the previous few appointments with her, we knew she was very sympathetic and understood how, for this close family, the ground was going to give way after this diagnosis. Both Maninder and I understood at the same time that the consultant had to communicate in a detached way to soften the blow. She gave us some time to absorb the sudden shock of being told that there was no proven cure for this form of cancer, then she went over the options available in terms of treatment, without going into detail about the uncertainties inevitably encountered during and after treatment.

I used to take Amarjit and Maninder to the hospital for his regular intravenous chemotherapy and clinic appointments. The sight of misery, fragility and death staring from the patients in the waiting rooms there used to fill me with deep foreboding. A sudden pall of depression would descend upon me. The very air in the hospital reeked of helplessness, mortality and the sepulchral closeness of death haunting many of the stricken people there.

15th June

The chemotherapy sessions slowed down the growth of Amarjit's cancer, but could not coax it to go to sleep. Oncologists decided to give Amarjit a stronger dose of chemotherapy. We were aware of the side-effects of this secondary chemotherapy treatment, but there was no alternative. Soon after the treatment was over, we discovered that Amarjit's bone marrow had been severely impaired. He would need a stem cell transplant in a Birmingham hospital.

5ᵗʰ August

The gruesome stem cell treatment in Birmingham only gave him a temporary relief from the ravaging cancer. Its looming presence did not recede much, though it slowed down for a few weeks. After a couple of months, the para-protein count in Amarjit's blood started to rise again. The oncologist gave him some chemotherapy tablets with devastating side-effects, such as the loss of hair, frequent nose bleeds, incessant pain in legs and feet and a complete loss of the sense of taste. Amarjit, at times, felt delusional as if he were experiencing an alternative life. It was very upsetting for Maninder. I focused on supporting her as best as I could.

The fear of what was going to happen soon was immobilising and she spent all her time fixated on what she had to do without thinking too much about the bleakness that lay ahead.

II

——————

The sudden discovery that he had cancer made Maninder and everyone else in the family very worried, but not without hope of an eventual course of successful treatment. They all thought that with new treatments of chemotherapy and radiotherapy, the disease would be cured and Amarjit would be back to normal before long.

Amarjit did not give up paid work, even after his formal retirement. He took on a part-time job three days a week and often came back home shattered and in need of immediate bed rest. His whole life had been given to working hard for his living and it was heartbreaking for it to come to a halt and for him forego his routine. Without any extensive hobbies, he did not want to feel life had made him redundant, an irrelevant entity. The need to work and work hard was ingrained in him. He believed working was his call of duty that he must heed.

31st January

After Puneet's death, I hated all festive occasions. We used to celebrate Diwali at home, a small ceremony, thanking God for the blessings bestowed upon us. We used to have some token sweetmeats, light candles throughout the house and enjoy a sumptuous vegetarian meal. There were always tiny spasms of excitement in our bodies and words came out of our mouths, dancing their way to each other.

But that was when Puneet was with me. Now I dreaded the thought of celebrating Diwali. I did not want anyone lighting fireworks, to send any Diwali greeting cards to friends and candles in every room at home became a distant memory. I loathed Christmas and the New Year gave me nothing but dark, melancholic thoughts about what I had lost.

To my horror, I sometimes resented watching other people enjoying themselves while I was sinking. Maninder's presence though was gradually changing my perspective; she brought hope, brightness and warmth to the icy landscape of my despair.

I felt increasingly more and more optimistic about life. Puneet was adamant in the days leading to her final moments that I must do everything possible to live life to the full and not spend all my time sinking in hopelessness. Maninder reminded me of the promise that I had given to Puneet and I said that I would do my best to carry out her wishes.

I felt good after Maninder had gone back to her house and felt convinced that life, though plagued by endless aches and pains, might have something more wholesome to offer, too. The fear about Christmas and the New Year receded in the background. My closeness with Maninder suddenly became an essential part of my thinking and, more importantly, it was untainted by guilt.

10th August

I come from a Hindu background, being born into and raised by family where Hindu customs and traditions played a significant part of daily life. Going to the *mandir*, my mother fasting during Karva Chauth and inviting five girl-children from the neighbourhood for lunch was a common sight at home. My father used to recite *shlokas* from scriptures without any books in front of him. We were, however, a Hindu family primarily in name only. There was virtually no distinction between different faith communities in the village. I did not have any thoughts about different faiths or castes constraining my mind.

I imbibed many key elements of our family faith, such as the role of karma, the presence of divinity in all living beings and the desire to seek emancipation from the cycle of birth and death. I was, however, not very comfortable with many rituals routinely undertaken by followers of my family faith. The quest for *moksha* also did not resonate with me. Was there a first-hand account we can rely on to subscribe to the theory of transmigration of soul? Has anyone ever sent a postcard from above after death to give us a clearer picture?

The most significant element in my childhood was the positive relations between people of different faiths in our village. We just got on with one another without delving into people's faith backgrounds. It was not unusual for me to go to a *gurdwara* with friends and listen to the recital of scriptures with respect and attention. I had a number of relatives who had spouses from Sikh family traditions.

Maninder came from a family of Sikhs where *maryada* was observed as a matter of course. But not to the exclusion of other faith communities. Her parental family was part of the village community and took an active part in all the shared activities. Inviting Brahmins to lunch, going to Shiva's *mandir* in Garhshankar, going on a pilgrimage to one of the temples of the Hindu goddesses up in the mountains – it was all done as part of her family faith, without any demarcation between different religions.

Both of us had a strong belief that it was only through erasing false distinctions between faiths that could we ever aspire to true integration. Both of us had learnt to focus on the individual because, in dealing with others, there could be no other criterion that might determine our judgement about people en masse.

10th November

Amarjit's health deteriorated at an alarming rate. Some days, he felt he was on way to recovery, but, more often than not, he felt all the energy seeping out of his body. The regular treatment to augment his platelets and low blood count would leave him devastatingly weakened.

We knew that the prognosis was not very good and that, after the second round of chemotherapy and then stem-cell treatment, there was not much hope left to cling to. Palliative care alone was the next step set out by his consultants. The spectre of death could be seen advancing slowly but inexorably, but we found it impossible to envisage such a sudden end to an otherwise active life.

14th April

After a period of long and hard thinking, we decided to get 'married'. Not a traditional marriage, rather a spiritual bond. We only wanted to exchange vows to support, to reaffirm our sincerity and loyalty to each other in a holy setting. Even though we were not very religious in terms of observing rituals, we played with the idea of going through the marriage ceremony in a *gurdwara*. I decided to do that in deference to Maninder's family background. We approached a *gurdwara* in a nearby town and the designated member of the management there, to my utter bewilderment, said that our plan was not practicable.

On a sunny morning in late March, we went to the local *gurdwara* along with some friends to witness the *laavan* ceremony. As we entered the main hall, there were around thirty or so young Sikhs in rather intimidating traditional Punjabi clothes sitting there chanting *Waheguru, Waheguru* at a furious pace. Most of them had *kirpans* slung over their shoulders. When the bride and bridegroom across different faiths arrived at the shrine, their entry seemed to give them a spur to raise the volume and speed of their chanting. When they looked at them, their eyes did not ooze any love or warmth though – they were simply glaring.

It was a very unnerving scene. I had read about the crusade against interfaith marriages in *gurdwaras* which was being actively promoted by a few ethnic TV channels.

The wedding ceremony we had gone to attend had to be cancelled as there were serious objections to an interfaith marriage in a traditional religious setting. Most of these objections came from the younger generation who had growing tensions with their parents and the older generation as a whole.

First-generation Sikhs who had migrated to the UK were anxious to fit in with mainstream society and they were willing to modify some of their faith customs as a result. The younger generations, particularly those who were involved in Sikh politics, were anxious to assert Sikh essentialism and keep their doors closed to any variations. Ironically, in India, interfaith marriages still do not raise any dissenting eyebrows amongst ordinary members of the public.

We came back from the *gurdwara* feeling slightly deflated, but not dejected.

A ceremony is not much more than a ritual, is it? Wedding ceremonies are performed in places of worship in front of holy books, devotional music is played and played again, sermons and exhortations delivered to impress the value of marriage on the bride and groom, but, as soon as the ritual is over, most of those participating in the religious part of the event retire to a banqueting suite to celebrate by consuming vast quantities of alcohol and meat – both of which are prohibited in a place of worship where older people with management responsibilities rule the roost.

That very day, we decided to do our own private ceremony. We decided to exchange vows of loyalty, faithfulness and enduring love for each other.

Maninder came to my house in the late afternoon a couple of months after having witnessed the thwarted attempt by two people obviously in love to go through a religious ceremony. She had brought a shawl which had been a gift from her late mother with a red *phulkari* design on it. She also brought with her a burnished gold-coloured suit with her as she knew that was my favourite colour.

I made some *parshad* in the kitchen, a sweet offering commonly found in a *gurdwara*. She brought with her a couple of holy booklets.

We sat on the floor and offered prayers to God and all the associated deities. I applied a bit of red powder just above her forehead. Offering prayers brought a tear to my eye and seeking divine support for our togetherness was very therapeutic. We had a simple meal after the ceremony was over and felt that our union was now embedded in our lives. I knew that she was still married to Amarjit who had been suffering from a worsening back pain for quite some time and that they had led a contented, peaceful life, but the sudden rising tides of love had swept both of us off our feet. The informal ceremony, without any ado, somehow cemented our relationship and I vowed to keep her family honour intact.

Since our tryst that afternoon, we began to feel more secure, more confident and much more self-assured when in each other's company. We did not have any witnesses at the ceremony, but we knew that if there was a Supreme Soul up there, we were going to be accountable to her/him.

Keeping our love private was an all-consuming task. We had to be extremely vigilant when in public, Maninder and I – whenever we went shopping in Dudley or to one of the neighbouring towns, we kept our distance and had rendezvous only at times agreed beforehand. I was aware that no one was going to blink an eye if they saw me with a woman, but it was entirely different in the case of Maninder.

They would lose no time in putting together two and two and making five.

12

Amarjit could not survive and his departure meant an abrupt end to my sense of continuity. Even while he was seriously ill, I still regarded my home as a sanctuary with a belief that he would not let me come to any harm. He was my ultimate defender, my shield, my guard without whom life had lost much of its meaning. It took a long time for his loss to sink in and, when I realised that he was no longer there to safeguard me, or to give my life a sense of stability, I felt bereft and completely disempowered.

The funeral rituals took up a lot of my time and, with my family and Shivraj's help, I managed to send him off with dignity, according to the rituals and traditions of my faith. His ashes were immersed in the flowing waters of India. Saying goodbye to him and screaming within, I found myself sinking in despair. Shivraj supported me by not merely saying words of consolation, but through taking on the organisation of the myriad funereal rites.

The ensuing mourning for my loss was a dark period in my life. I struggled to find any ending to my internal suffering. The visits by dozens of relatives, people from Amarjit's village and friends, did not provide any escape from the cloudburst of uncertainty in my mind. Visitors came and mouthed some clichés and offered vacuous platitudes, rather than focussing on the way Amarjit lived his life or how he provided timely support to his friends in times of need. I remember him telling me how he used to take bags of corn to someone whose parents lived a life of destitution and could not make ends meet. The elderly woman from his own clan in the village that he supported had a son who had migrated to England and was then settled in Halesowen. After a brief stint in a factory, he became a primary school teacher. His teaching was constantly attracting negative comments from his pupils and colleagues though. At that time, it was well-nigh impossible to get rid of a teacher as the procedures for sacking someone on the grounds of incompetence were protracted and enervating. At the time of Amarjit's death, Pritam, the old woman's son, was seriously ill with some kind of terminal disease which they did not want their friends to know about. His wife, Gulshan, came twice to join the group of mourners, but chose not to speak even a single word of consolation to me.

During my married life, I did not experience any frenzied periods of excitement, except when I saw my mother after ten years on my first visit to India from the UK. It was a meeting that both of us found too emotional to express it, even through sobbing utterances. It was love, pure love, unselfish love, helpless love and nothing else. That encounter, after having spent just over ten years in England, separated from each other except for the occasional broken telephone conversation, seared my whole being and I was oozing love, sheer love for my mother. In England, there was nothing that made my heart beat faster though, but I did not miss that because I had seldom experienced occasions when one's heart waltzes with joy. Nonetheless, life, despite its banalities was calm, steady and without any serious disruptive episodes. Both of us were doing manual work, but it brought in the money to give us the wherewithal to provide quality care for our family.

During Amarjit's life, I remained blissfully unaware of the responsibilities of running a home. I focused on keeping a clean house, feeding my family, bringing up my children and going to work. Amarjit took on the responsibility of dealing with the outside world, paying bills, getting repairs done or ensuring no greedy relatives or people from his village disrupted our peaceful life by their frequent, unannounced visits. After his death, the burden of dealing with the outside world fell upon my shoulders and added to my stress. The tending of the garden which Amarjit used to look after now seemed to be an impossible task. I could not even distinguish between weeds and burgeoning new plants at times.

A couple of months after the mourning rituals were over and friends had almost stopped coming over to offer their condolences, I had some space to take stock of my life and feel grateful for the life I had lived so far. The visitors, after the initial five minutes, would often start talking of things, news or happenings completely irrelevant to my situation. For example, they would start talking about politics in Punjab, news of other friends and their own families or even about television programmes. My mind would remain totally disengaged and their words did not lessen my pain.

A couple of my former colleagues kept me company, supporting me and exhorting to be brave and to do so for the sake of my family.

When Satinder, a former colleague, but now a friend, visited me again after a couple of weeks, her eyes were glistening with tears. I got worried because I had always found her to be a courageous, uncomplaining woman who went about running her house and looking after her family assiduously.

Her litany of ill treatment by her husband, Kewal, was the thing I least expected to hear when we got talking. She gave me a catalogue of incidents when she had been at the receiving end of venom, vituperative hostility and even mind-numbing physical abuse. Kewal had had a manual job in a foundry when they got married. She came from family where fractured relationships were the norm. Her father had deserted her mother and got a second wife in his village in Punjab. Her brother, who had been living in England, could not sustain a stable marital relationship with his wife and, a few years after Satinder got married, they decided to part company. Satinder did not have anyone else from her parental family in Brierley Hills she could call upon for advice or support. She found herself at the mercy of her husband who was consumed with toxic disregard for her from the very outset.

In the early days of their marriage, Kewal would flatly refuse to take her out shopping or to the cinema. Even when they had three children, he would show nothing but dismissive disdain if ever she asked him to go on an excursion or a picnic.

She would not be allowed to visit her distant cousins in Coventry, unless she paid for the fuel in the family car.

Kewal, almost illiterate and completely alienated by any intellectual pursuits, would often rage against her at mealtimes, complaining the food she had cooked was over- or under-salted. To show his dissatisfaction, he would hurl his plate of food away or smash it to bits against the nearest wall of their living room.

Satinder had no one to turn to for advice and she felt she was alone without any family support and, if she resisted, she knew she would be thrown out of the house. So, she put up with Kewal's coarse heartlessness in silence, venting her grief in the privacy of her bedroom.

They were living in separate rooms in the same house and their paths rarely crossed. But now Kewal was seriously ill. His stomach decided not to aid the digestion of any food he cared to put into his mouth. His visits to the local hospital became more and more regular and Satinder took on the job of taking him to his appointments. Even while languishing in his medical afflictions, Kewal did not show any remorse or any acknowledgement of the huge effort being made to look after him. His refusal to mellow down was the heavy burden she found so difficult to carry. She wanted to share her frustration and unrequited feelings with me.

I felt stunned and had utter disbelief about the horrific treatment she had to accept in silence. I tried to soothe her and Satinder found the listening time I had given her helpful. In contrast, I was thinking of Amarjit and his caring attention to my well-being. I could not recall even a single incident when he ignored my wishes or became oblivious to my need for encouragement and support.

I began to see Shivraj almost every day for advice, guidance and to seek his help in doing the essentials that I had to take on. He took care of the legal matters relating to probate, changing the will and associated legalities. He took time off work and I was relieved that he knew what to do and, more importantly, how to get things done in the aftermath of Amarjit's death.

The more frequent contact with Shivraj not only made me more dependent on his support, but also brought us closer as it rebuilt my self-confidence. A new umbilical cord had emerged and his presence became a lifeline for me.

Along with that, feelings of love and tenderness towards Shivraj began to bubble up in my thinking. Conversations with him on every subject that weighed upon my mind became a necessity and were ultimately cathartic. I found his presence soothing, warming, invigorating and increasingly an antidote to depression.

Two people, mature, past their prime, but enriched by life's varied experiences, supporting each other sounds very normal, almost natural. But, in Indian society in general and in Punjabi society in particular, it is something to be regarded as a heinous crime. The treatment given to widows or divorcees in the traditional Punjabi society, particularly amongst the immigrants of the first generation, is nothing short of a scandal, a cancer that no one has dared to face up to.

The community of which I was a member expected me to forego my right to live as an individual without any rights to dignity, happiness or even life. A widow is expected to stop wearing good, colourful clothes, make-up or go out shopping, except in the company of her children. I was reminded of the ashrams in Vrindaban where widows ostracised by their families live a life of penury, sheer deprivation, routinely becoming de-sexed creatures, but also are subject to lewdness from men with wandering eyes.

Menfolk in the traditional Punjabi patriarchal society might have illicit affairs without any qualms, but if they saw a widow living a decent, dignified life they would be foaming at their mouths, passing unsavoury comments in whispers and resolving to keep their distance from her. Widows are deliberately "uglified" by their clothes and the absence of jewellery or make-up to deprive them of their femininity. I witnessed some of Amarjit's siblings change their attitude towards me. I ceased receiving telephone calls from them or any expressions of interest in how I was coping with my grief.

The void in my life, the sudden shock of losing someone who had provided care and warmth all through our married life and now the constant subterranean hostility and indifference from one's own family and friends made living harrowing.

Shivraj, however, was always cautioning me against the pitfalls of the traditions so slavishly followed by the Indian diaspora. It took me more than a year to become disenchanted with the mores of my own community. While I was still being cautious, I was getting more and more rebellious about the reactions of people who had little respect in my eyes. All I wanted to do was to live my own life, on my own terms, and retain my self-dignity and independence.

There was a yawning wide chasm between the way Shivraj and I had been brought up. I was born into a family with a farming background, grounded, down-to-earth, not given to articulating emotions, but one always focused on providing security. There was little higher education in the family, although one of my brothers managed to go to university which helped him find a good job in the irrigation ministry.

I had led a sheltered life all through my marriage.

But now I had to take on the responsibility for maintaining my home entirely on my own. A frightening, mammoth task which filled me with fear and apprehension. I had a job too that did not bring me into contact with life outside my home – that being how to deal with wily relatives, how to ensure all the household bills were paid on time, how to deal with the extensive network of people from Amarjit's village who had migrated to the Black Country – it was different terrain for me to traverse. In my lonely hours now, I found myself in a bewildering no man's land. Shivraj's guidance, advice and willingness to take on tasks made life so much easier. I was in a constantly learning mode, but his support incrementally gave me enormous self-confidence.

Living with one of my sons was not an option that I could even begin to seriously contemplate. I had seen many friends and acquaintances who went to stay with their sons when they lost their husbands. Each one of them, without many exceptions, discovered they had lost their independence the moment they left their own home. They were invariably at the mercy of their daughters-in-law who regarded them as an additional, dispensable burden. They were treated as creatures without any individual needs. They became redundant appendages to their children's family.

One of my closest friends, Seema, decided to stay with her son when widowhood was thrust upon her by a car accident. She used to be decisive, capable of making her own choices, meticulous in her planning, but when her husband's death compelled her to leave her house and move to her son's house in Warwick, she became increasingly confused, indecisive, and somewhat mentally unhinged. She became her son's family's cook, nanny and housemaid. After a few years, she became psychologically an imbecile, unable to make up her mind about anything, a sad ruin of her former self.

I wanted to avoid a similar fate at all costs. I wanted to retain and guard my independence.

There were several aspects of daily life that challenged my exploratory skills. The garden soon became a magnet for unruly weeds and, when I ventured out timidly with a fork in my hand, I discovered that I was not very confident about distinguishing between weeds and plants. I had to learn everything from scratch, how to battle with the moss that liked to find its resting place in the lawn, how to tame the lawnmower and how to define lawn edges.

I also found it difficult to manage the house that Amarjit and I had over the years substantially extended. It was not only the matter of keeping the rambling house clean and dust-free, but also the inevitable loneliness that it evoked within me when alone. I was familiar with every nook and corner of the edifice, but there was something missing that made the familiar house ask me questions that I couldn't answer.

"Where do people go after they die?" was a recurring question which tormented me. The belief in reincarnation, karma and the determination of destiny by someone watching over the universe – nothing really consoled me or mitigated my anguish. Shivraj had a few years earlier gone through a similar experience though.

Hence he was able to offer me insights into his own experience, without any recourse to dogmatic beliefs. The confusion, sense of bewilderment, the tidal waves of grief engulfing the mind – he was able to afford me a peep into his own grief. And I found that his experiences gave me a bit more clarity than merely listening to clichés or platitudes.

The prejudice and the unexpressed, but still-in-your face hostility that most people of my community had in abundance for me gave me many a sleepless night to start with. Amarjit's own cousins and other motley relatives who used to be so full of warmth induced by fake affection had turned their face away from me now. They would have welcomed the sight of me crumbling under the crushing weight of my bereavement. They could not bear to see me going about the business of living in a calm, orderly manner. Many of them knew it was Shivraj who was providing me with the confidence to face the world without falling apart. And they hated that. I was not acting like a suitable recipient for their sympathy.

Since all my children had left the nest and fond jobs away from Dudley, I could not have readily accessed their support from a distance. Shivraj lived only eight miles away and could reach me within minutes if I needed help urgently. Our meetings became more and more regular and every day we would meet up and talk, eat, laugh and sometimes cry together.

Looking back at those dark times, what stands out was the sheer luck of finding someone at my age and stage in life who could hold my hand, offer unselfish support and remain as my North Star in the firmament of life. This relationship restored my hope in life and gave me a desire to relish the precious days that I had left on the planet.

13

Jaswinder set off from his home town of Banga as if floating on air, his heart full of dreams. His ageing father, Amar, and mother, Baksho, had led a life untouched by affluence or plenitude. They owned a small holding, about 1.5 acres, just outside their town and Amar spent much of his time ploughing, sowing and harvesting there. The income generated used to be barely enough for their family to survive. Jaswinder was their only son and their daughter, Sukhi, lived not far from Banga with her husband and their two children. Jaswinder did not have any passion or desire for education and spent much of his time doing nothing but playing cards with his friends after he had left school.

In the farming community that Jaswinder came from, working on the land was usually considered to be below one's dignity. However, he was a member of the Jatt community, which traditionally eked out its living by working on farms.

Even so, there was, at that time, an influx of cheap labour from Bihar, Utter Pradesh and Bengal all over the state and the indigenous young people felt that getting work done cheaply was a boon to the society there. While the newcomers from other states toiled and worked hard to improve their financial position and send money back to their families, many young Punjabis couldn't think of anything better than passing their time drinking alcohol or taking drugs, which were readily available. Feeling stoned without a break of full consciousness became their addiction and their parents, despite constantly wringing their hands and blaming the drug suppliers, could do very little but to watch their sons dying a slow death. The law enforcement agencies were merely bystanders due to the involvement of some corrupt politicians in sanctioning the contagion of drug addiction.

Amar and Baksho were desperate not to have their son commit a slow suicide by taking to drugs. The only thing that could save Jaswinder was for him to go away from his village, preferably thousands of miles away and get used to the idea of working hard for his living.

In Phagwara, a city a few miles away, Jaswinder and some of his friends came into contact with a travel agent who offered to send them to Germany from where, he assured, they could easily proceed to London and be subsumed in the crowd of illegal or over-stayer immigrants. He also assured them that they could easily find work there, which although mainly manual, would get them lots of rupees to send back to India.

Apparently, London was awash with money and people did not have to struggle too much to amass a fortune, according to the travel agent.

Like the rest of his gang, Jaswinder felt very excited at the prospect of living a life of luxury. He persuaded his father to sell off his holding which fetched about £3,500, enough to pay the agent his commission for making it possible to realise his dream. He was getting intoxicated at the very thought of having lots of money, finding a suitable girl to marry and living in a big city.

On a warm, sultry day in September, he boarded a flight along with two of his friends, which, he thought, would take him to Frankfurt. On disembarkation, he discovered that the flight had landed in Tripoli instead. All of a sudden, a manic fear gripped his heart when saw the mayhem not far from the airport. There were hordes of agitated young men milling around with guns and foaming at the mouth, shouting in a language he did not understand. Even though his knowledge of geography was very poor, he knew that Colonel Gadaffi, Libya's dictator, had been mercilessly killed after having spent decades marauding the landscape and undertaking sexual exploitation on a catastrophic scale. The ensuing riots and lawlessness, plus the surge of Muslim extremists from neighbouring countries were some of the things he had read about in the Indian newspapers.

Fear stalked his every moment of consciousness and even crept into his sleep at times. Jaswinder and his two friends had to hide when some Islamic State jihadis offered to take them to Mosul where they could work in an armament factory. They had seen the headlines in the Indian newspapers about the barbaric atrocities committed by ISIS fighters in Syria. They had also seen the macabre videos of Jihadi John delivering his vitriolic speeches before beheading his captive prisoners.

Jaswinder and his friends went into hiding in deserted buildings, amongst the ruins of shops and houses. They went without food for days and often lay there silent, trying hard not to make a sound whenever they thought Islamist extremists were roaring outside.

During a brief lull, they slowly headed for the sea to see if they could get out of Libya. A local agent offered to organise their transportation to Italy if they were willing to pay an additional exorbitant sum for their boat trip. They had no means to procure that kind of money. The only way to escape, they thought, was to go subterranean and bide their time to seek a boat which could take them out of Tripoli. It took them more than four months to find a rickety boat and the crew promised to take them to Italy if they parted with whatever money they had in their possession. They boarded the boat, exposed to the perils of the sea, famished, without food for what felt like several days.

On reaching land in the dark after midnight, they disembarked and wobbled towards the shore, jaded, lifeless, dying for something to eat and drink. Soon, they found themselves in a different country. Instead of reaching Italy, they discovered to their dismay that they had arrived in Malta where it was impossible to find any regular work.

It took Jaswinder and his friends over six months to reach England on the back of a freight lorry. Exhaustion and malnutrition had claimed the life of one of his friends soon after they had left Malta. Jaswinder found his way to Tipton as his father knew some people from Banga who had settled there in the early sixties. He came into contact with hordes of illegal immigrants like him and, due to their networks, he did not have a problem finding a labouring job in the construction businesses. Most of the builders he was working with were of Indian extraction and they were willing to hire *faujis*, as the illegal immigrants were called, on a daily basis, paying them way below the minimum wage. He worked seven days a week and tried to visit the local *gurdwara* on a daily basis to partake of the free food, *langar*, available there.

Jaswinder knew that since he did not have any papers to legitimise his stay in England, the only recourse was to find a girl who was already legally entitled to live here. He dreamed of finding someone who could, in time, make him a citizen of this country, able to live without any fear of being caught.

He worked in a variety of jobs – as a washer-upper in an Indian restaurant, packing chicken carcasses in a factory and building tarmacadam drives. After more than five years, someone from his village who was regarded as a family friend, complained about his illegal stay to the immigration authorities. He was apprehended, but released to await the processing of his application for over-staying and was asked to report to the police in Solihull once a month. He had already spent seven years in the country with little chance of visiting India to see his parents. He felt desperate to find someone who could rescue him.

One of his distant aunts, Bhinder, was in Stourbridge and she was approached to seek a legally settled girl for him to marry. Bhinder was a close friend of Balbir and was aware of the mess Kirti was in through Ranjit's desertion. Bhinder decided to be the go-between and approached Dalbir with her proposal. A couple of meetings were hastily arranged for Kirti and Jaswinder to meet up for a chat. While Jaswinder was oozing out excitement, Kirti couldn't sustain any conversation or stop her tears rolling. She felt she would be unable to give herself to anyone after her betrayal.

Jaswinder was persistent and showed considerable tenacity and hope, pledging to care for her in the days to come. Kirti's reluctance to accept his proposal of marriage took many months to be overcome. Maninder had worked with Bhinder in Stourbridge for many years and they lived in the same neighbourhood. Bhinder brought in Maninder to counsel Kirti not to reject the opportunity for stability in her future life. Although she was fully aware of the subterfuge underpinning their wedding proposal, Maninder found it very difficult to constantly see Kirti writhing in pain for no fault of her own. Kirti had lost faith in the sincerity of all males and was not willing to choose a partner in India for him to join her later in

England. She was content with her job in the factory, spending time with her former mother-in-law, Dalbir. Her deep sense of betrayal had made her a regular reader of the holy books of her faith to seek solace.

Dalbir and Maninder spent hours with her reminding her that life without a partner was going to be very lonesome and strewn with problems. She accepted their suggestion to meet up with Jaswinder. She didn't find him appealing as she was still haunted by past memories, but eventually she relented and said yes to the proposed marriage. They underwent a simple religious ceremony at the local *gurdwara*, followed by a small reception in a nearby pub. The whole thing was subdued, flat and without a single increased beating of her heart.

Married life, however, remained bland, bereft of any excitement or joy, and she worked hard to try to spend as little time with Jaswinder as possible.

Living in the Black Country, doing manual work in a factory close to the Bentley Bridge shopping centre, without any friends who she could trust and light years away from the carefree surroundings of her village, Kirti felt suffocated, as if trapped under a heavy rock after an earthquake. Suppressing her loneliness and desolation and doing her best to be oblivious to the displays of mirth and happiness she saw while shopping or going to work, she felt she could either implode with grief or go insane. The whole world around her seemed to be going about its business as usual and there was no one who would pause and feel sorry for her.

The drudgery of daily life continued to grind and, slowly, she discovered she could find some uneasy peace only in living a parallel life. They were living in the same apartment, but their intimacy did not extend to anything beyond that. Sometimes, their paths crossed, but she had the shield of chagrin and indifference saving her sanity. Being two strangers living under the same roof suited her and somehow calmed her angst and eruptions of resentment against the raw hand destiny had dealt her.

Years went by. Jaswinder's application took ages to be processed, at times being deliberately left on the shelf due to the vociferous noises made by UKIP and some other right-wing politicians against immigration from the European Union. She chose not to have any children until Jaswinder got the go-ahead for approval to have permanent domicile in the country.

From time to time, Kirti used to visit Maninder, pour her heart out and have a good cry. She had severed her links with old friends or members of Ranjit's family. She felt disempowered, totally helpless and tried to lose herself in the monotonous chores of running her rented apartment and not to think about the mirage that life once seemed to tantalise her thinking.

Maninder knew she couldn't do anything to mitigate her misery, but her readiness to listen was therapeutic for Kirti.

Jaswinder worked with a construction contractor who had employed many undocumented immigrants from the Indian sub-continent. He knew he could expect blood, sweat and tears over long hours from his crew, while paying them ridiculously low wages. He was working on a road-building project a few miles outside Worcester. The contractor used to send a van to transport the crew to the site of work every morning at 6 o'clock and arrange their return around 8 in the evening.

One winter morning, when it was still dark and a thick layer of fog was spread-eagled over the landscape, a lorry driven by a Polish driver on the motorway ignored the roadworks signs, ploughed through traffic cones and hit a couple of workers who were busy removing debris onto a forklift truck. The lorry screeched to a halt and the ensuing sound of the collision caused a lot of scampering, running in blind panic and wailing. The lorry driver, who had momentarily fallen asleep at the wheel, woke with a start and sat in his seat with his eyes glazed and a puzzled uncomprehending expression. Soon after the accident, the workers rushed to where the lorry had juddered to a halt and discovered that the two of their co-workers had been badly crushed in the collision.

The police arrived within a couple of minutes of the accident, along with multiple ambulances, with sirens blaring and paramedic staff. They had the gruesome task of taking the two injured workers to a safe place on the hard shoulder. The whole area was convulsing with noise and people talking in delirious tones. Soon, it was established that one of the two people bearing the brunt of the accident was Jaswinder. He was immediately taken to the Worcester Acute Hospital, but despite the best efforts of doctors and surgeons, he died soon after arrival. He had a cracked skull and had fractured his lungs and legs. The severe injury to his brain made it impossible for him to regain consciousness. He was declared dead while still in a coma.

Kirti couldn't believe the enormity of her shock. Despite leading a parallel life and not having any intimate relationship with Jaswinder, she felt herself hurtling down an abyss of emptiness and endless pain. She had hardly got over the withering pain of treason dealt out to her by Ranjit and now the sudden snatching away of Jaswinder tore her life apart. She had not enjoyed married life for more than a few months and now she found herself single again. She couldn't go back to India as she knew the widows were the bottom of the heap there, completely ostracised by society and regarded as a fair game by predators. She had reached the point of no return and was not willing to be subjected to stigma and ignominy.

14

I was deeply saddened by the latest cruel blow that Kirti suffered. Having been once rejected by Ranjit, she had no choice but to marry Jaswinder, despite nursing a smouldering, bruising sense of betrayal. She did not want to set her eyes upon another man and was happy living on her own with her former in-laws. She was not oblivious to the fact that her current status quo could not last forever though. Ranjit had moved out his parents' house and she was nothing more than a burden, which his parents accepted to atone for their sense of guilt. It was they who had organised her wedding, having secured Ranjit's acceptance, when they had gone over to India to look for potential brides for their son.

Kirti was not a bad-looking girl, being slim, reticent, bashful and not acquainted with Western modernity in her daily life. Despite her belief in gender equality, she had seen her father having the final say on all important family issues.

She had not come across any conflict or friction between her parents and always found her mother supporting her father in a willing and even enthusiastic way. The fact that she was away from her familiar village environment made her rather timid and instinctively withdrawn. She looked to Ranjit to make almost all the decisions in their newly set up home. Her prime responsibility, she felt, was to please her husband and win his trust.

She had fair skin, much-prized by the Indian community. Her skin was punctuated by tiny bits of acne though which you could discern only when close to her. Many celebrities in India could be seen on television advertisements promoting assorted creams and lotions with magical bleaching powers. This was a legacy of colonial rule as people equated fair skin with power.

Kirti was living a simple life in her village in India and little things, such as playing with her girlfriends, listening to Punjabi music and reading manageable chunks of scriptures and being in the company of her parents made her happy. She had been living in a protected milieu at home and was not exposed to the outside world in a social context. The occasional visits by close relatives and the frequent unobtrusive visits by neighbours did not really involve her, except for exchanging pleasantries and responding to their routine questions about her schooling. The world outside the home and in the cities eluded her as if there was a thick curtain separating them. Kirti did not, however, miss any interaction with the outside world. She was in a cocoon; the feeling of warmth and cosiness was enough to keep her contented.

Kirti was an avid reader and often borrowed them from the library at school or the public library when in town. Her reading of Sikh scriptures, the poetry of Amrita Pritam and Shiv Batalvi and the novels of Nanak Singh and Jaswant Singh Kanwal instilled into her a sharpened awareness of the gender inequality in the hierarchal society in her village. However, her awareness and perceptions were mainly shaped by books which she used to read on sultry afternoons when going out in the blazing sun did not exercise any pull on her. In her daily life at home, she did not find any covert discrimination in favour of her brother. Ideas of independence and equality, though very abstract, held a strong appeal to her thinking. She found the whole concept of gender equality exciting and dreamed about witnessing it in her world. She had some views which struck a chord with me in terms of gender equality or the centuries-old denial of rights for women in the traditional society around us. Sometimes, she found it difficult to articulate those views, but her mind was, nevertheless, brimming over with ideas which militated against the routine repression meted out to girls in the Indian society.

England, to her, was a land of equality and social justice. She hoped to see some sort of equality in action in her adopted home after marriage. When she landed at Heathrow and headed to Dudley, she expected to see women having a strong voice, but soon discovered that the Indian diaspora had brought over the same traditional attitudes and concepts and made strenuous efforts to fossilise them. The freedom given to boys in Punjabi families, while, at the same time, keeping an unforgiving, vigilant eye on girls were the sort of things that irked her sensibilities. She felt, however, helpless, caged without any say or hope to change anything.

Kirti's views on the need to recognise women's issues resonated with me. That was one of the reasons why I felt the need to offer her support. It was the least I could do for her.

I confronted Ranjit at a wedding reception, which both of us were attending.

"Why did you decide to leave her?"

His response was utterly vague and gibberish. He said without any conviction in his voice: "I left her because Kirti did not get on with my friends and remained embarrassingly unsociable."

He did not tell me that he had broken off with Kirti because he was carrying on with Samantha. Kirti could at least look after the house, keep it immaculately clean and take care of cooking. She was more than happy doing chores for Ranjit, without asking anything in return. Samantha, on the other hand, could not look after even her tiny council house. The rooms in her house were full of clutter, the floor strewn with empty fast food containers. She could not be even bothered to look after her own appearance. Her children from previous marriages were unruly, untouched by any discipline or structure. But Ranjit chose not to say anything about

Samantha when he stopped by our table for a few minutes to say hello.

I knew full well that Jaswinder was no match for Kirti, but there was no other option available. She could not have lived in Ranjit's parents' house forever. She could not spend her entire life visiting the memories of the time immediately after her marriage to Ranjit. So, I encouraged her to consider spending the rest of life with Jaswinder. I knew Jaswinder had over-stayed his visa in England, but he had been living and working here for many years. There was hope he would be granted permission for a permanent stay as was the practice for many generations of illegal immigrants.

Jaswinder was a short young man, smartly dressed when not at work, and had youthful looks. Even though he had lived in this country for almost nine years, his grasp of English was still not firm though. He was a man of few words and, after he had been introduced to Kirti, he fixed his gaze upon her face and she instinctively turned away to avoid eye contact. Later on, whenever they visited my house to have a sort of rendezvous, it was interesting to watch them sitting for minutes without uttering a word. Much of the talking had to be done by me.

I also knew that that my arguments in the end gave Kirti the confidence to take the plunge, despite her reluctance to do so. The sudden tragedy when Jaswinder was mown down by a sleepy lorry driver was something no one could predict. I felt a huge sense of loss and wanted to support Kirti yet again. Life had been very cruel to her, but it was time to move on and live her life for herself. She could not spend the rest of her life sunk in the morass of her personal grief. I knew from my own life that the pain of personal bereavement is not always responsive to the passage of time. From time to time, it has the habit of undergoing an eruption and scorching the entire mental landscape yet again.

In the following weeks and months, I invited her to my house regularly and shared many conversations and peaceful silences during our time together. I felt grateful for the opportunity to avoid loneliness that was chasing me after Amarjit's death.

Amarjit had been very kind to me – plain, simple, reassuring, steady, without any fuss. Life with him was akin to homecooked food, wholesome, but not always something to write home about. After his death, the sudden vacuum that yawned in front of me was frightening. I felt very grateful that Shivraj was already on the scene to fill that vacuum. My relationship with Shivraj could not have made any headway if we hadn't known each other for more than twenty years. We did not have an occasion to talk at length on any issue or spend any time together to share our thinking on life and the world around us.

I am bemused when I recall how I even found it difficult to look him in the eye, I was so used to avoiding looking at his face, even when talking with him. It was all out of respect as in my culture staring at someone often symbolises something less than that. But I knew Shivraj was kind, a man with a big presence and enormous confidence. And we had fallen in love with each other, even before Amarjit was diagnosed with cancer. Puneet's death had filled Shivraj with so much anguish and pain that he couldn't regain his self-confidence. I could see that he was like a star that had fallen out of its orbit. I couldn't leave him alone to fight the demons of his pain and I believed it was my duty to support him until he was back to his usual self.

Amarjit's final days were full of relentless anxiety and desolation. Constant nose-bleeds and fatigue that refused to go away, flagrantly disregarding anything that was being done to address it through medication or physical care, occasional episodes of hallucinations, the sudden appearance of rashes over his body, sporadic incidents of forgetfulness and retreating into his past – every day the signs of deterioration were becoming more and more alarming. He was still oblivious to his prognosis and the inexorable deterioration of his faculties added to his bewilderment. I did not have the courage to tell him about his imminent conclusion of his life on this planet. Finally, I had to ask the local hospice doctor to have a word with him. She was very tactful, but delivered the message in a subtle but transparent way. A sudden pall of gloom descended upon Amarjit and his eyes glistened with tears. From that moment on, he became more and more reticent, unable to talk about anything that worried him.

Some of his relatives in England came to visit him regularly, but I had to be mindful of the risk of him catching an infection. His immunity levels were virtually non-existent and I had to incur the wrath of his brother and sister when I asked them not to sit in his room, particularly if I suspected they were even slightly suffering from a cold.

Amarjit's end came peacefully. It was early in the morning and I rushed through my daily routine to be by his bedside. I asked him if he was suffering from any pain. His eyes were closed, but a very faint, muted gesture of his right hand told me that he was not. His face looked peaceful – his big journey out of this physical world had started. I was holding his hand and whispering *mool mantar*, the Sikh prayer. I felt he could hear my voice and probably understood what I was saying. He opened his eyes wide once before his breath became shallower and shallower and, within minutes, he breathed his last. Kulwinder and Devinder came later on that morning after Shivraj contacted them.

While we were busy with the arrangements for Amarjit's funeral, his brother, Mukhtar, began to make remarks, very casually, about the need for someone from his own family to take on the responsibility for the funeral rituals. In a way, he was being critical of the involvement of Shivraj in the aftermath of this death. Such barbed comments, not always subtle and even bordering on being uncouth, became more and more common in my bereavement. But there was no one else who was willing or able to liaise with multiple agencies to ensure a fitting farewell to Amarjit.

One of Amarjit's relatives lived in the nearby town of Brierley Hill. Some fifty years ago, he'd landed on these shores as a visitor, but never went back to India. He did a stint of work in a factory for about ten years and then went on sick leave complaining of severe pain incessantly triggered by lumbago. Since then, he had been living on state benefits and had refined the art of getting around loopholes and maximising the financial support he could squeeze from the state. After ten years of marriage, he was frustrated that his wife had not produced a child. To him, it was a cardinal sin that she had failed to present him with a child who could continue his legacy and bear his surname. The easiest course, he thought, would be to find another wife. He went back to India and got another woman – a distant cousin of his first wife. He was able to go on annual holiday to far-off places with both his wives as they, in turn, were also claiming disability allowances. He was shrewd enough to divorce his first wife on paper to make his second marriage legitimate in a legal sense. They, however, continued to live the same house as a happy family, with a rota system in place for spending nights with the wives.

He came to visit Amarjit during his final days and spent his time pontificating about politics, morality and faith. Making grand statements about the world and the way it was being run. I asked him not to tire Amarjit out by talking so much. It was obvious to me that he was offended and pronounced that Amarjit should have made an effort to enjoy his life, without spending it all working hard. Leisure pursuits would have prolonged his life, he suggested. I decided not to let him come to violate Amarjit's calm with his wordy, but meaningless pronouncements.

The funeral was a sombre experience, giving me a new perspective on life. Here was the man who brought me over to England, who gave me financial security and acknowledged my choice to bring up my three children and run the house. Although most of his relatives were obnoxious people who loved to get his extra pound of flesh, he had shielded me from their reach.

I had experienced most of my adult life only with him and that had made me comfortable and secure. Before marriage, I had an intense desire to pursue further studies, but living in England without the support of my extended family got me busy with the mundane chores of daily living. The desire to pursue further education had slowly fizzled out and the only reminder left were the few letters that I once wrote to a friend in India about my frustrations at the prospect of giving up my studies to get married.

That was many moons ago though. With Shivraj's help, I felt I was able to walk again with a sense of purpose. I was convinced that my time on this earth, too, might be short and that the need to make the most of what was left was my only responsibility. Shivraj was instrumental in cementing within me the new realisation about the fragility of life and the urgency to live life as my own person with inviolable rights and entitlements. The exhortation that I got from him was the reason for my giving support to Kirti. I did not want her to spend her entire life slowly dissolving in sorrow.

In the Punjabi society in England, that was easier said than done. Young men looking for a bride here would not cast a second glance at someone born in India, especially someone who had originated from the hinterland of the Punjab without any social etiquette or social skills to interact with the mainstream society here. She would neither contemplate bringing a potential husband from India because (a) she had to be in a job earning the minimum as laid down in the then immigration regulations and (b) after having spent many years in this culture, she felt someone raw and new from India would be a misfit, a relic of another world. I had to counsel her to consider Jaswinder as he sounded like a nice, reasonably educated young man from Jullundur. Moreover, he came from the same background as Kirti, a Sikh family given to hard work and reading scriptures every day and visiting the *gurdwara* regularly. Jaswinder ticked all the boxes, except that he had not yet received permission to stay indefinitely in the country. There was hope though that, by dint of his staying in this country for almost a decade, at some point in the future, he might get that elusive approval.

Following the tragedy of losing my husband, I found myself in unremitting darkness, without any hope of seeing a ray of light. The world outside the home was an alien place for me. I needed someone who could overcome the barriers put up by Punjab society which did not give any credence to the value of women, a society which has been rigidly patriarchal for thousands of years. I was already in love with Shivraj, though maintaining my loyalty to Amarjit. My slightly platonic love for Shivraj did not exclude my duties towards my family. It rather strengthened my resolve to be a good mother and a supportive wife. My mind was with Amarjit, even when my heart had given itself to Shivraj. After the funeral, I found myself in the wilderness in terms of my dealings with my relatives. They did not turn their back on me, but the pronounced shift in attitude they had undergone was palpable to me.

Once I was attending a social event when one of the elderly female cousins said to me. "Maninder, the colourful clothes that you are wearing don't suit you. People are bound to say that someone who has lost her husband should wear simple, preferably while garments to indicate continued mourning."

At a wedding that I had gone to attend, Baksho, the gnarled, stunted woman from Amarjit's village, cornered me. "Maninder, how are you since Amarjit's death? I hope you are spending much of your time reciting scriptures, remembering Waheguru, God and not bothering about attending too many weddings."

Amarjit's family members in India began to salivate at the prospect of taking possession of his agricultural land in the village. They were obsessed about finding out how much Amarjit had left behind for me. I resolved to sever all links with those relatives and cast them out of my mind to avoid frequent bouts of hurt and depression.

I often thought about Kirti and the injustice meted out to her perturbed me. She did not find it possible to cast Ranjit out of her mind, despite his deceit and naked betrayal. With hindsight, one could see when the rot set in. He started going out with Samantha whose council flat was not very far from the garage where he worked. Inevitably, he began to drift from Kirti and would find flaws in everything she did or even she didn't do. Samantha was an extrovert and Ranjit was not her first trophy, whereas Kirti remained bashful, reticent and gave the impression that she did not have any refined social skills.

Although she got on very well with his parents, she became a recluse, focusing on mundane things, such as cleaning, cooking and occasionally visiting the temple with Dalbir. She never could find any room in her heart for Jaswinder. He was spending most of his time at work, labouring for a series of contractors who liked to employ undocumented immigrants and pay them minimum they could get away with. Jaswinder was promising her the earth and stars because his sole purpose was to legalise his stay in England. That would have helped him to bring over one or two other members of his family from India.

The accident on the motorway where he was working was a tragedy, but it did not fill Kirti's heart with impassable sorrow. His loss, however, increased her conviction that she was destined to live a life of isolation in utter misery.

15

Amarjit had inherited some agricultural land from his parents in his ancestral village. That piece of land had been in the possession of his younger brother who had died a few years earlier and was now being cultivated by his nephew and his family. Amrik, his nephew, had hired some Bihari immigrant labourers to cultivate the land and he made his living selling the produce in the market town of Phillaur. Amarjit had not received even a single penny out of that land. I raised this issue with Amarjit on a number of occasions and asked why he was not doing anything to reverse the squatting rights of his nephew's family and sell the land off.

"We are definitely not going back to that village to live for more than a few weeks. Our children have absolutely no interest in moving back to India either."

"No, I can't imagine selling that land, it is the legacy of my ancestors. Besides, what will people in the community say?

That I am selling land to sever my links with my roots!"

As if that was not good enough a reason for his inertia, he would often say in a soulful tone, "Perhaps I might decide to settle in my village after I have retired."

Nothing happened. After some time, I pushed the issue of selling the land to the hinterland of my mind. Amrik and his family lived off the proceeds of the land and sometimes asked for money to be remitted to them for improving the land, such as having a bore well for irrigation, or for hiring a tractor to plough.

After Amarjit's death, I decided to sell the land and distribute the proceeds to my three children. I had no desire to go back to his village or see his nephew's family. Their two sons were addicted to hard drugs and spent their days and nights in a daze or inflicting violence on their neighbours or people against whom they happened to nurse a family-inherited grudge. The nephew's wife, Sharan, spent her time getting garish, but expensive garments made or constantly eating food and drinking juices and smoothies in enormous quantities. To call her chubby would have been a very kind, diplomatic statement!

Selling land if you do not live in India is akin to climbing a steep mountain with a tight string around both feet. You have to grease the palms of innumerable people to get anything done. First, the deeds and the boundary of the land had to be prized out from a minor official, *patwari*, who demanded a bag full of money before he could even begin to consider the request to look into his records. Then the documents obtained from him had to be ratified by district officials who demanded their pound of flesh. After spending a couple of weeks doing this, you had to cross the next hurdle. The power of attorney had to be ratified and approved by a registrar who sat salivating in his air-conditioned office. If you couldn't find someone influential to persuade him to stamp and sign your papers, you had to offer another bag full of rupees to massage his ego. Then there was the hassle of finding an agent to seek out potential customers, haggling over the price and the inevitable wait for weeks and weeks after. It took me two visits and knocking on countless doors, but eventually I managed to sell that little bit of land. I tried to forget the torturous hassle of form-filling, getting everything ratified by an accountant, trying hard to propitiate the bank clerks before I could transfer the money to England. The incessant pressures and the constant rush of adrenaline, along with sleepless nights, made me unwell on returning home. My health unsurprisingly began to suffer. Hypertension, frequent bouts of insomnia and a toxic sense of frustration were busy gnawing away at my mind and I felt I was losing interest in the world around me.

My salvation came through Shivraj who helped me regain my self-confidence and his constant support incrementally erased the dark memories of my experiences in India. Shivraj did that through talking, playing music, reading poetry and taking me out of the cloistered environment at home to enjoy the breathtaking beauty surrounding us in the countryside.

Walking through the park with a light drizzle on our faces, Shivraj would talk about the deceit he had suffered from in his distant past. He talked about the sudden morphing of some of his own relatives into monsters after his father's death. He often talked about the nadir of his life when his wife was caught unawares by cancer and how her loss irrevocably changed his perspective on life. His comments and advice were invariably sombre, philosophical and the result of the life he had lived and was still living. But he was also full of humour and would regale me with an alliterative use of language, often disjointed in terms of meaning, but ridiculously rhythmic in delivery.

There were some mild arguments over our divergent views on a few issues though. With Amarjit no longer beside me to take on the running of the house, I became sensitive to the mundane pressures of daily life. If anything went wrong in the house, I became slightly panicky, whereas Shivraj, despite living on his own, was calm and a bit laid back in his reaction to things that sometimes were prone to going awry. My biggest worries came from my garden. Whenever I saw any weeds growing merrily in the borders, I would recoil as if they were denizens from another galaxy. The difference between plants and weeds eluded me as I had not previously ever done any gardening. If there were any brown flecks on the leaves of my acers or philadelphus, I would break out in a sweat and lurched towards trowels and forks as if fighting a deadly virus.

Shivraj was always busy counselling me to stay calm and enjoy whatever little gardening I could manage. Although he was not an avid gardener unlike Amarjit, he knew instinctively what to do. He had recourse to books and gardening blogs to refine his knowledge of plants.

In the chaotic years during Amarjit's terminal illness, I got used to neglecting myself. I was not eating well or on time and would often fill myself with stale, barely inedible food cooked quite a few days ago. Shivraj, on the other hand, was always keen on freshly cooked food. He used to spend hours asking me to prioritise my own appetite and not to treat it as something peripheral.

When I was young, I used to have a burning desire to go for higher education, but since I had to leave my dreams of studying further and come to England, my dream had slowly withered. All of my time was spent on looking after the house and my children and the thought of reading books slowly, but inexorably atrophied. My desperate wish to go to university receded in the fog of time. Shivraj tried very hard to rekindle my old love for education and would often bring me books and magazines to read. However, I found it very difficult to reignite the dying embers of my dreams. Perhaps that part of the brain that nurtures curiosity had gone into a prolonged hibernation.

The biggest upheaval I experienced since Amarjit's death was that I found myself exposed to all manner of what I perceived to be predatory situations. Making sure there was sufficient money to pay the bills, keeping the house in good repair, looking after my own health and sanity, doing my duties towards my children – even minute mundane tasks seemed to be impregnated with unseen, lurking dangers.

Shivraj became my pillar of support, my North Star, someone I could rely on come what may. We drew closer and closer to each other and I increasingly became oblivious to the potential caustic judgements of my relatives and community. I was still very cautious and did my utmost to go a long way to avoid the attention of the first-generation Punjabi people around me, but mentally I found myself becoming stronger and stronger. While many members of my community had no sway on the way their own children decided to choose their partners, they were, nevertheless, keen to make acerbic comments about other people. Nothing would give them greater delight than watching an older person die of loneliness, depression and a broken heart. I was determined to deny them the opportunity of savouring that pleasure.

16

My neighbourhood in Dudley had a concentration of people of Punjabi origin who had made the streets there their home. The demand for houses there was insatiably high as new immigrants from the Doaba region in the Punjab were drawn to that area.

There were a number of reasons for the influx there, but mainly it was about safety in numbers. There were strong threats from irate members of some right-wing members of the white community who were vociferous in expressing their anger about the rising numbers of immigrants in their country. They did not want the culture, mores and texture of their life changed by people speaking other languages and following strange customs and traditions.

Secondly, the newcomers had a great deal of anxiety which diminished when they found that they did not have to adapt to the new life here in a hurry. They could survive in their part of the town without having to learn English. They could easily do their shopping in cornershops where Punjabi was the language of communication. They could go the neighbourhood place of worship, pray and choose not to mingle with the seemingly hostile outside world. They could easily procure the latest Bollywood videos and watch their favourite stars on their VCR machines. In case of physical threats, they could summon help and just about make life bearable.

Things underwent a complete change in later years when their children grew up with a fervent desire to be part of the mainstream community. But for the first-generation immigrants, being in a silo was better than being exposed to the unknown fears prowling outside around them.

Many of such immigrants were living in dire poverty though they measured the depth of their deprivation against what they had experienced in India. More than a dozen people often lived in a terraced house, sleeping in one bed in shifts, cooking out of tins to keep hunger at bay and working all the hours they could manage – it was all a blight afflicting their lives. And yet they were happy because they had escaped real poverty in their motherland, where even earning your bread was a challenge, where jobs eluded them and where the only consolation they could find was through their faith. They had the unquestioning acceptance of the inevitability of kismet through their faith traditions. They toiled, sacrificed their own needs to support their families in India and prayed for better days to come.

When I arrived in Dudley, I would find many of Amarjit's friends and colleagues congregating around a tape recorder listening to Punjabi songs with a nostalgic mist in their eyes. Soon after my arrival, Amarjit bought a black and white television set in the first terraced house that we had purchased. Although I found it difficult to understand the lyrics, I found myself drawn to the music of Beatles, Gerry and the Pacemakers, Freddie and the Dreamers, Petula Clark and later on Tom Jones and Englebert Humperdinck. "Green, green grass of home" reminded me of the safe nest that my parents had lovingly built for me in the small village that once was my home.

Starting a new life in a new country was a massive, sometime daunting, challenge for me. I did only rudimentary cooking as I had not gained those skills in my adolescence. In my new home, there were many comic mishaps in the kitchen when I was experimenting with cooking different dishes. Cooking lentils with all kinds of assorted vegetables thrown into the pot produced dishes seldom seen or revelled in by mortals. While intending to make soup, I would be miserly with the water and end up serving gloop in a bowl to Amarjit. Vegetarian dishes, which were meant to be dry, would have pints of water added to them with the flotsam of different bits having a merry wander in the soupy concoction. But Amarjit never complained about my cooking. Gradually, I watched and learnt the art of cooking from others though watching them in their kitchens. Watching *Top of the Pops* with a bowl of cauliflower and potato *subzi* swimming in a puddle of soup was somehow quite soothing!

Mark and Susan, our next-door neighbours in our first house, had a very tidy garden. I had been to my parents' farm which was only metres away from our house in India, but, nevertheless, I had absolutely no knowledge of the plants or flowers growing in our neighbours' garden. They had a small patch in their garden for growing vegetables. They used to give us a few flowers or produce from their vegetable patch from time to time. One day, while Amarjit and I were in the garden, Mark gave a few stalks of rhubarb over the fence. We thought the stalks were saplings of an exotic plant that we should put into the ground. Amarjit dug a hole, I filled the hole with some mulching leaves and both of us carefully planted the rhubarb there and said a little prayer for it grow nicely. A couple of days later, we again bumped into Mark who, while exchanging pleasantries, said: "How did you find the rhubarb? Did you enjoy it?" Although we did not fully understand what he was saying as he was speaking too fast for us, we knew instantly that perhaps we should not have planted the stalks into the ground. All we could say was, "Oh, yes, we are still watching it with interest. It looks healthy." Poor Mark had a puzzled look on his face!

Gardening was a new experience for both of us, particularly for me. One morning, Amarjit took me out in the garden and asked, "What would you like me to plant in the garden?" I instantly said, "Why don't we plant some sugar cane, maize, turmeric and ginger in the soil here. Then I can have sugar cane juice in summer and use ginger and turmeric in my cooking. And I love munching on roasted corn cobs," Amarjit scratched his head and, after a few minutes, said, "I don't think these things will grow here. It is not very hot here, we spend most of the year shivering in the cold."

I was happy though and did not miss sugar cane juice or the vegetables that I was familiar with in India. Over time, the fragrant memories of mustard *saag*, cane juice, maize *roti* faded away and I became comfortable with whatever was available in my new home town.

I missed having walking shoes, the kind I used to wear while going for a stroll in our fields in India. Amarjit did not know much about ladies' shoes. He took to me a shop which looked very pricey and posh. We bought a pair of designer stiletto shoes for £99. Amarjit's weekly wages did not extend to even one third of that amount of money. When we came back, I spent some time calculating how much £99 would be in Indian rupees. I was horrified and did not have even a wink of sleep that night. The very next morning, I went back to the shoe shop and exchanged the designer shoes for two pairs of plain shoes.

The fact that both of us were learning new things at the same time was comforting.

Since I was feeling secure and safe at home, I did not miss even the Bollywood films that I used to be fond of while at college. I did not miss those film starlets who used to have such a huge following amongst the girls there. I got used to watching television programmes here and although the dialogue was not always comprehensible, I became enamoured with the background scenery and music and caught onto the broad contours of the plot. After the birth of my three children, I began to feel that England was my home and that there was absolutely no need to look back.

We made quite a few visits to India, mainly to feed the insatiable appetite of greedy relatives with presents from here, but emotionally I realised I was drifting away from my nostalgic past. My affinity with India lasted as long as my parents were alive. After their death, there was no emotional pull to visit the country. My visits thereafter were only to accompany Amarjit who had not lost his emotional pull for his folks in Punjab. I used to make sure I did not spend much of my time in his ancestral village and usually went to see my brothers' families in other parts of the country.

17

4th June

Religious intolerance was spreading like an evil unstoppable virus. Maninder and I went to Paris for a weekend. It was Maninder's first visit there. I have long been an admirer of the culture, architecture and couture of Paris. It has always been one of my favourite cities as the pace of life there is civilised, the cuisine wonderful and, although some Parisians are reluctant to admit they can speak English, it is a city easy to navigate. We were admiring the sights and stopped by Notre Dame Cathedral to fill our eyes with the grandeur of the stained glass windows. The place's history overwhelmed all our senses and evoked an irrepressible sense of awe and wonder.

As soon as we came out of the building, we could see a lot of commotion, with tourists hurrying to escape and a heavy presence of police. We discovered that an extremist Islamist, born in France, but originating from Algeria, had tried to hit a policeman there with a hammer. Due to the rising tide of terrorism by followers of a sect that set out to establish a Caliphate in parts of the Middle East, most public places increasingly witnessed stepped up security. The attacker was promptly shot dead by armed police. There was cordon placed around the cathedral, but after a long wait, we were allowed to make our exit from the building.

When normal daily life is so violently and abruptly disrupted, it casts a shadow over your mind for the rest of the day. You cannot take safety for granted – that was very clear to us and the loss of freedom, we felt, was something to mourn.

29th June

The sun is ablaze in the sky and I am sitting in the garden watching butterflies frolicking around a fragrant bush. The flapping wings seem to be almost stationary due to the incredible energy and speed of their movement. The sky is almost blue, a rare scene here. While I am watching the snowy clouds slow-dancing across the firmament, I cannot help but think of the paradise that I lost a decade ago. Puneet used to fill my whole being with sudden surges of delight, the way she walked, the way she talked and, above all, the way she looked. Her face used to radiate innocence, warm, unconditional love and a mellowness not often found elsewhere.

A sudden howl rises to a crescendo through my heart and the surrounding lushness around me is instantly gone. I look around, but find nothing to engage my focus.

After a few minutes, I return to the reality of the present and think about Maninder who came into my life to lift me out of the morass of grief. Although she sometimes has a fiery temperament that impels her to make sharp statements, much of time she is soft, caring, loyal and considerate. It was she who has made my loneliness recede gradually over the years. Now I find that my grief over Puneet's passing away is in a secure compartment of my mind, taken out from time to time, but, much of the time, kept there as a reminder of the heaven that once I inhabited. Life now is tolerable, even enjoyable and often ignites hope and dreams – all because of the support I am getting from Maninder. I am working very hard to make her life more comfortable, particularly in her bereavement, but I know I am nowhere as effective as she has been to me.

15ᵗʰ July

England has been my home for many decades and I feel I am making my contribution to mainstream society here. Yet, in moments of stillness sometimes when I am half-awake, nostalgic memories of my childhood and adolescence in India surprisingly spring forth in my mind. The faces of my mother and father who died years ago come to reside in my eyes and I can see them vividly as if they were, here and now, with me. Each and every furrow, wrinkle, tic, smile and the ocean of love and warmth in their looks comes alive. The way they talked, gestured with their hands to emphasise certain points, the sounds they made when clearing their throats to hide their emotions when meeting up after a gap of years – the whole panoramic experience fills me with warmth and a sheer longing to have a chance to see them once more grips my heart.

Life is very brief though. When my parents died, they were the same age as I am now, in their late seventies. Disobeying joints, the sudden descent of tiredness, an awareness of the preciousness of the short time left before I join them, all this and many other memories flock to my mind, giving me a strong reminder of the fragility of life and of the need not to take life for granted.

When Maninder talks about her parents, of the distant childhood memories in a village where no more than a dozen families lived, of the unstoppable love filling her mother's eyes – we have a strong reminder that the only recourse left to us is to be committed to our care for each other.

10th August

Extremism is on the rise. There are tragic episodes being reported day in and day out in many countries. Here in England, we can witness the inexorable rise of a hardened, brainwashed version of religion in many communities. Young males, though not exclusively, are going back to a distorted interpretation of their scriptures espoused by preachers. Their high-octane hatred for other faiths is driven by an irrational grievance against the world. They are convinced that all the powers in the world are pitted against them, determined to annihilate their beliefs and subsume them in their decadent way of life. The assault on the Twin Towers in New York and the explosion of bombs on the underground in London signalled that this spiralling down was now almost unstoppable.

Darshan, an old acquaintance from Brownhills, tells me that he spends all his time watching one of the Sikh channels on television and continues to feel outraged at the atrocities meted out to Sikhs in Punjab. He fulminates against the chief minister of that state for turning a blind eye to the endemic disrespect shown towards Sikh scriptures and places of worship. I am taken aback because, during the last forty years since I have known him, Darshan has evinced absolutely no interest in the political developments in Punjab. He moved to Brownhills over fifty-five years ago and did not go back there, even on a short visit, for the next forty years. Since the introduction of some religion-based television channels though, he has become more and more convinced that Sikhs are soon going to be an endangered species. He has been to India many times during the last five years and, on return, has brought with him many anecdotes to corroborate the rumours and analyses offered by often illiterate presenters and premonitions about the imminent crisis facing the whole community.

He took illegal possession of a tiny piece of land next to

the house that got built for his family in his village in Punjab. The village council forced him to demolish the ramshackle boundary of bricks that he had built around that piece of land. Darshan was adamant that he had been discriminated against because he was a turban-wearing Sikh and that the authorities in India were systemically targeting his community.

The transformation of a peace-loving acquaintance who was having nightmares about the precarious future of his community was not a total surprise, but, nevertheless, a shock to me.

18

Kirti was working in the kitchen, preparing a *dhal* for the evening meal. Dusk was slowly descending upon the landscape and the slowly fading light of the day reflected her mental state. Desolation didn't accurately describe the feeling gripping her shattered heart. Am I going to spend the rest of my life cooped up in this Calcutta hole without any hope of watching sunlight touching my face? Ranjit had dealt her a cruel blow and, after the initial disbelief, Kirti had begun to feel a surge of anger against him filing up every artery, every pore of her body. If he was not serious about marriage, why the hell did he come over to India to choose me as my life partner? Why undertake this subterfuge? Why this deception? She could not fathom the depth of deceit and depravity in his mind.

She was seething like the bubbling saucepan in which a yellow *dhal* was happily shedding its hard shell and yielding to softness. She turned on the light and a weak glow reluctantly came from the single light bulb which had not ever enjoyed the company of a lampshade.

Suddenly, the telephone rang.

"Hello. *Sat Sri Akal*," she whispered.

"*Sat Sri Akal*, Kirtiji. My name is Tarsem, you probably don't remember me, I met you briefly at Aunty Maninder's house when I was visiting her a few days ago. You will remember that Aunty Maninder introduced me to you. I am from her extended family. Her cousin Satnam's grandson is married to Billi who is a distant relative of my brother."

Confusion was running riot in Kirti's mind.

"Sorry, I do not understand why you have rang me. My *dhal* is boiling over and layering the top of my cooker."

"Kirtiji, I was wondering if I could see you soon as I have something urgent to tell you."

"What do you want to discuss with me?"

"It is difficult for me to explain over the telephone. Please do not worry, I would love to have only a few minutes with you."

"Give me your telephone number please and I will try to get back to you." Kirti was anxious to end the call. She made a note of the number and put the phone down.

The whole evening, she felt restless. She did not know what to expect and how she should have responded. But hearing a male voice of someone who was not related to her was not an unpleasant experience. She had a sleepless night. Should she ring him or should she put a kibosh on the whole incident? She found it difficult to make up her mind.

The next morning, she could not resist ringing Tarsem on his mobile and ended up promising to go to the cafeteria at the local Woolworth's with him.

Tarsem did not mince his words. He had taken a fancy to Kirti. There was this childlike innocence that had captured his heart. He was vaguely aware of the tragic events that had battered and bruised her life, but he confessed he couldn't get her out of his mind since he set eyes upon her ten days ago at Maninder's house. He could recall every detail of the circumstances that brought him face-to-face with Kirti. He was at Maninder's house to give her a box of Indian sweets as his brother in India had become the father of a baby son for the first time. Kirti was already there having a tête-à-tête with Maninder.

The following days and nights passed in a haze of euphoric sensation. After thinking for a long time, Kirti felt she could consent to meeting Tarsem again to listen and, perhaps, talk.

Tarsem was a well-built young man, older than Kirti by four years, and his appearance showed he was not suffering from financial deprivation. He was running a taxi business, hiring out taxis to drivers who paid part of their income to him in lieu of paying a rental and getting bookings through his base where a he had a couple of telephonists on duty twenty-four hours a day. He had eight drivers and the money generated by them included the hiring cost of the vehicle in addition to 20% of the fares received. Tarsem did not have to do any work himself other than ensuring the taxi business operated smoothly.

About four years ago, he'd got married to Amrita, a Punjabi girl from Oldbury, born and bred in this country. Sabbi, an old woman in his neighbourhood who loved being a go-between, had brought the two families together. They had a lavish wedding, booked a banqueting suite and hired a DJ who specialised in playing ear-piercingly loud Bhangra music. More than 500 guests had crammed into the hall and gorged themselves on the huge number of dishes prepared for the occasion. There was vigorous dancing in front of the hall and the guests were taking out fivers and tenners, circling the notes around the wedding couple's heads and leaving them for the DJ and his accomplices. Although there was a huge variety of meat and vegetable dishes, together with *naan* and pilau rice, most guests targeted the whisky bottles left on the tables. They were downing it as if it was the only time they could appreciate scotch, with lots of water and other mixers.

The first month of their married life had hardly ended when his bride, Simi, told him that she was already in love with another young man who attended the same College of Further Education as she did. The revelation came during a showdown when Tarsem confronted her and asked her why she was constantly trying to avoid him in the bedroom. The sourness between them increased by the day and they had nothing in common to discuss. When they were together, there was an eerie, cold silence between them and they were frantically trying to make smalltalk about topics that did not matter to them at all.

The gulf between the two became so wide that they decided to part company. The revelation that Amrita already had an intimate relationship with another man was too much for Tarsem to bear. The very things about her personality which used to capture his fancy had taken on a much darker hue. He started to feel a sense of revulsion when they were in the same room as if the mysterious person who had been close to Amrita were there as a barrier. Within a month or so, Amrita went back to her parents' house and, before long, they filed for a divorce.

Kirti was a tonic in his life. She had had two failed relationships in her past life, but as she had to forego them under circumstances beyond her control, this made the situation more bearable. Tarsem knew she was not at fault, but it was her destiny that she had to align with those two unfortunate souls. Perhaps her destiny was to be with him, something preordained by their stars.

Their meetings continued with increased frequency. Kirti was initially very reluctant, almost sceptical and unwilling to open up. But Tarsem's persistence gave her the confidence to pour her heart out and share her anguished past and the newfound joy of their meeting. Within one year, they got married at a very simple ceremony. They sought blessings from Maninder, touched her feet in deference and asked her to be their chief guest at their wedding. Their wedding took place in Himley Hall, followed by a sumptuous meal. Maninder stood in for Kirti's parents during the ceremony. There was some live music by Miss Pooja, a well-known Punjabi singer.

Once they were together as a wedded couple, they purchased a bungalow outside Stourbridge and lived a life which could be termed as quotidian without any storms raging through it. Over the following five years, they had two children, a boy and a girl, and they spent all their spare time bringing them up, surrounding them with care and love. Kirti in time half-forgot the traumas she had suffered with Ranjit and Jaswinder. The pain that had been eating away at her soul was slowly loosening its tight grip. Tarsem became successful in his business venture and had a large number of very loyal clients who trusted him much more than Uber. On their wedding anniversary, they would visit Maninder's house to have her blessings renewed and to thank her for being instrumental in bringing them together.

Ranjit and Jaswinder completely left her mind. The travails she had experienced in the past became a distant memory. She was still inclined to be reticent when it came to expressing her happiness or love of her new life, but the way she took on household chores and the important tasks of bringing up her children had infused a new energy into her steps. At times, it seemed she was walking in a charmed trance.

As the years rolled by, Maninder and Kirti drifted apart. It was not possible to maintain regular contact with each other and that's what Maninder had wanted all along. She wanted Kirti to enjoy a fulfilled life without feeling beholden to anyone, including herself.

19

Shivraj often says that I go for the company of obsessive worries. Yes, I know that I worry too much and about too many things. If there is anything that needs doing, I get restless and, if delayed, it overpowers my mind. Shivraj, on the other hand, is blissfully laid back and more relaxed about the chores that we have no choice but to perform to live a tidy life. I often wonder why he doesn't worry about the unruly shrubs in his garden or the cleaning of his windows or the pile of ironing that await him. I think he does have all these tasks as priorities, but minus a sense of urgency. He likes to bury his head in a book or journal, rather than dust things in his lounge.

I wasn't always like this though. Amarjit used to take on many of the tasks concerning the running of the house. Any repairs, gardening, the paying of bills and cleaning the car – all this was his territory. My job was only to ensure there was cooked food on the table and even with that I used to get help from him.

As a matter of fact, I even learnt how to cook from friends or Amarjit's female relatives. There were hordes of people from his village who had settled in the Black Country and we used to have regular, unannounced visits from them. I used to get tips about cooking from the women who used to visit us, along with their husbands and children. I remember once I made a green pepper dish, with a generous helping of water to make it soupy and sprinkled it over with the seeds from the peppers for decoration. I knew instantly that I had done something which was not right when I saw everyone avoiding eating that dish, which is called *subzi*. When the guests had left, a non-stop volley of burps convulsed from my stomach. When Amarjit told me that he had not come across my version of the green pepper dish ever before, I knew I had to take some action. I asked an old woman who had originated from his village where I had gone wrong and soon the penny dropped.

During my first pregnancy, I developed a sudden craving to have something sour, sharp and fairly hot. Mango pickle from the Indian shop fitted the bill. I thought it would be good idea to make mango pickle *subzi*. So, I sautéed some chopped onions, added ginger and a liberal amount of garlic, along with the usual spices. When the paste was ready, I drained half a jar of mango pickle into the saucepan, added some potato chunks and cooked it for an hour. When Amarjit arrived back from work, I placed a big bowl of pickle *subzi* and some chapattis in front of him. He took a bite and then said: "Maninder, I don't why I don't feel very hungry today." I felt slightly deflated that he had not appreciated my cooking skills. It was only when I tried to eat it that I realised cooking mango pickle was an insane idea!

The same sort of naiveté was abundantly clear with regard to plants. I didn't know the names of most of the plants in the garden as they all looked pretty much the same to me. I wasn't used to having a garden at home in India. Fields, yes, with various crops that I could recognise, such as sugar cane, mustard, some common vegetables and orange trees – that was just about as much as I knew about farming. When I saw Amarjit pruning our overgrown shrubs, I used to worry that they might be feeling hurt.

Some of the weeds which I took to be plants were growing wildly, such as couch grass and bindweed. I thought their sudden spurt of growth required additional nutrition. So, I started to water them after sprinkling on some plant food to give them a boost. No wonder some of the weeds went berserk, like the beanstalk in the children's fairy tale, their growth spurts being accelerated by the day. It was only when Amarjit started moaning that our garden was a safe house for some nasty weeds that I realised that perhaps I shouldn't nurture them so much.

Since Amarjit's death, the responsibility for looking after the garden fell on my shoulders and, after a spell of bewilderment, I began to research the names of plants. Gradually, after a spell of trial and error and some forgetfulness, I began feeling quite familiar with the plants, shrubs and trees in the garden.

It was a steep learning curve, but it gave me confidence and contentment.

Living in that part of Dudley where there was a concentration of people originating from the Punjab presented its own challenges. After Amarjit's death, since I was living on my own, that raised many unsavoury questions in the minds of some local residents. "Why don't you go and live with one of your sons?" was the predictable question.

"Surely, your sons can look after you?" Or "Your daughter-in-laws are good and I am sure they will do everything to make your old age bearable."

Otherwise, there inane questions such as, "What do you do all day?" "How do you pass the time doing nothing?"

Most people from my community could not understand that I wanted to live an independent life, making my own decisions and not becoming a burden for my children. Independent living was a foreign concept to most of them. Funnily enough, many of those who asked such outrageous questions lived with their own children and were forever complaining about the treatment they received from them. They often talked about the acute sense of loneliness that plagued their minds, but getting out of the cage of traditional customs was not a task they could even contemplate.

One morning, I rang Satinder to ask about her well-being. She sounded very subdued and spoke in a melancholic tone. On probing further, she told me about the recurrent episodes of racial attacks that her family were suffering. Some youngsters from a family a few doors away had decided to throw stones at their bedroom windows, smash the windscreen of her car and woke after they returned from their nocturnal outings. She could not figure out what had triggered this sudden bout of harassment. It went on for three consecutive nights and the episodes were reported to the police but, without concrete evidence, they could not take any action.

In my case, it was a racial attack, vicious, remorseless and incessant. With things like this going on, the people of my own community found it difficult to see me having a life without having to knock on their doors for help. They could not understand how a woman, recently widowed, could have life of her own and not, metaphorically speaking, prostrate before the so-called elders of the community. To me, the very idea of seeking help from such people was abhorrent. In most cases, they could not sort out their own old age and lived a life of enforced silence as second-class citizens in their children's houses, but when they went out to while away their time in the market or park or a community centre, they would lose no time pontificating about other people.

One of my neighbours spent all his spare time prying into other people's lives, spreading unsubstantiated rumours to anyone who was foolish enough to listen to him. He breathed out sarin gas when talking about a widow in the neighbourhood who had the temerity to be seen in the company of a male friend. He was in his element when being scathing about older people getting together to combat loneliness.

"Can't they stay at home and recite God's name?"

"Why do they feel they are on fire in their hearts?"

When I had the misfortune to bump into him, I heard similar remarks and instantly knew that I, too, was one of the people who transgressed his "ideal" view of humanity. I could see him spending hours washing his family cars and, whenever an opportunity arose, pausing to have a chat about his grand design for the cosmos. I was aware of his poisonous sense of exclusivity because he revelled in sharing it with his neighbours or passers-by on his street.

Shivraj and I could not meet up freely without having to look over our shoulders because Dudley was full of Punjabis and many of them knew Amarjit. Actually, I was much more nervous than Shivraj when we ventured out. He had a healthy reaction to any unspoken comments from people because he had a lot of self-confidence and took pride in his achievements. His managerial role in the probation service had equipped him to prioritise his life properly. He did not have any time for superficial, ritualised, commonplace superstitions.

Over the next few years, I gradually, but determinedly, drifted away from Amarjit's relatives and co-villagers. They were not really bothered about my well-being or interested enough to find out how I was coping with my loneliness. The severing of the umbilical cord with Amarjit's relatives was a very liberating experience. I did not have to make regular telephone calls and pretend I was anxious to find out if their lives were running smoothly. The silence that ensued gave me an energising experience of calm, without having to chase the mirages of antiquated traditions.

I decided to go as far as possible from my old neighbourhood, which was infected with formalities, rituals, cultural entrenchment and laden with hatred based on deep-rooted prejudices against anyone who subscribed to a different outlook. After the move to Kidderminster, my suburban house felt like a haven of tranquillity, surrounded by nature in all its glory. It was on the edge of the town, surrounded by vibrant greenery. The locals' pride in keeping their homes and environment clean was obvious, whereas in my old street, it was common to see cars parked on the pavement due to residents who could not find a regular jobs and so mended cars on their drive. They were out there on their drives at all hours of the day, some Punjabi neighbours spending their time in their front tarmacked gardens, still in their pyjamas and long tunics. In my new setting, there was no prying, no twitching of net curtains and no spreading of baseless rumours. Perfect peace at long last and I thanked my stars every day.

One of my former neighbours, Mika, had migrated from the same village as Amarjit's. He came from a very poor family and his widowed mother did not have much land to eke out her income. Amarjit used to give him sacks of wheat, rice and lentils to keep their hearth hot. Mika married a woman who was not only the antithesis of grace and charm, but also very cantankerous, with a barbed, growly face. She was the daughter of a retired captain in the Indian army and Mika worshipped the muddy ground she walked on because he was overawed by her background. It was such a contrast to his own upbringing of continuous austerity. Over the years, Mika and his wife assumed an air of superiority because she had found a clerical job in the Inland Revenue. While Amarjit and I were still toiling and working in the harsh environment of a factory, they believed they were at a level of success that made them stand apart from the hoi polloi like us. Mika spent his life teaching Punjabi in various schools, being passed around as he was living proof that an ineffective teacher without a passion for raising the aspirations of children is universally disliked by their colleagues. I was glad that I did not have to pass their house in my new setting.

There were quite a few people on the estate who had been very close to me. We had gone through years of neighbourly amiability, helping each other in times of celebration or need. When my son, Dev, got married, I had two female friends who spent long hours in my house making preparations for the wedding, cooking for the hordes of guests who came visiting. I, too, reciprocated their friendship on their important family occasions.

However, when I look back at the number of people who were genuine, sincere and loyal, there were a whole lot more who were Janus-faced, sweet to your face, but harbouring an irresistible desire to be judgemental.

I did not miss the neighbourhood that I had left behind then. My formative years had been spent there, but everything went topsy-turvy after Amarjit's death. I was deemed to be a legitimate target for judgment by neighbours and relatives who were steeped in traditional culture.

"Why are you living on your own in such a big house?" "Why don't go and live with your sons?" "What do you do all day sitting all day at home?" "Have you thought about going back to live in Amarjit's ancestral village in India?"

Such questions became the refrain of many conversations and I could feel by blood pressure going up every time I had to listen to such uncouth, ill-informed remarks. In my new neighbourhood, I felt at peace, do I could afford to be still and meditate. What is more important, I could have Shivraj come to see me without any prying glances from neighbours.

20

Margaret lived in the bungalow opposite Maninder's house in Stourbridge. Maninder first saw her only after a month after she had moved house. She was old, but still sprightly, being quite fragile, but surprisingly full of verve and energy. She rang the doorbell and welcomed Maninder to her new neighbourhood. She must be over eighty, Maninder thought, marvelling at her smooth, flexible gestures. She gave an open invitation to Maninder to have a cup of coffee sometime. "What a reassuring neighbourly experience!" Maninder thought, planning to take her up on her invitation.

In her new neighbourhood, there were only a scattering of Asian residents and most of the neighbours were white, with the majority retired or semi-retired. The immediate neighbours did not wait too long before ringing her doorbell to welcome her and offering to help her, if needed. One of them, an old well-dressed man with a twinkle in his eye remarked, "We are a wicked bunch of people here, but you might like us as your neighbours."

A couple of weeks later, she went across the road to meet up with Margaret who was full of warmth, exuding genuine happiness about having her company. Her bungalow looked immaculately clean and the workshop that Margaret had created for herself was over-brimming with samples of complex embroidery and a number of landscapes painted by her in her spare time. There was a gardener in the front, taming the wayward shoots and branches of some bushes. He looked way past his middle age, but seemed diligent, gentle, with a sombre visage.

Margaret's husband, Rob, was in another room resting. He was eighty-eight years old and fragile, but determined to continue with his business in Shrewsbury. He visited his office once a week and, in his absence, it was either Margaret or one of their two daughters who attended to the office's demands. Maninder did not quite catch what precisely the business was all about, except that it involved importing goods from various European countries. They had a string of properties in Shropshire and Staffordshire they rented out. Margaret's lack of pomposity or ostentation struck Maninder and she warmed to her.

Margaret had a sparkle in her eyes and pursued her hobbies with vigour. She talked about her family and how she wanted to downsize her business activities, but Rob had stubbornly opposed any proposal to reduce their commitments. Maninder drank in the beauty of the bougainvillea splashing its grandeur outside the workshop window. There was a huge rose bush in a massive container by the patio door and its sweet, heady fragrance filled the entire room. She noticed that all the equipment in the room – the paint colours, easels, threads and fabric pieces were meticulously in order. Rob was fastidious about his food and unwilling to touch any "foreign muck". Margaret, however, loved the gentler versions of curries. They had a number of people coming in every week to clean the bungalow.

A couple of months had passed when, one day, Maninder suddenly realised she had not seen Margaret since their first meeting. She saw one of Margaret's daughters driving in and went across to find out if everything was all right with her. Melinda looked subdued.

"Mum hasn't been feeling too well lately. She's got bowel cancer and she's been in hospital for more than a week."

Maninder felt saddened. Although she had met Margaret very briefly, the sudden news about her illness hit her hard.

She would enquire about her recovery whenever she saw one of Margaret's daughters. On her return home from the hospital, Maninder rang Margaret. In the course of a short conversation, she mentioned how chemotherapy had damaged her taste buds and how the exhaustion assailing her was entirely alien to ordinary tiredness. She had lost a lot of weight and looked emaciated with a wan, weary look.

Amarjit had also experienced a similar loss of the taste of

food, she recalled. He was fond of eating good homemade food, savouring every morsel of what she used to cook. Eating *saag*, chickpeas and a variety of lentils with plenty of salads used to fill him with contentment. Chemotherapy, particularly the second round, had played havoc with his sense of taste though. He lost his fondness for food and ate very small portions just to survive.

Maninder set about making mild curries for Margaret and took them over to her bungalow. Rob who had never before deigned to taste curry, took a spoonful of chicken and potato curry and liked it so much that he rang Maninder to thank her profusely for her kindness. She looked forward to giving samples of her cooking to Margaret and a couple of other elderly neighbours. There was often a bouquet of flowers waiting outside her door with a nice message of thanks from Margaret. Whenever Maninder crossed the road to her bungalow to ring the bell, she would hobble out, unsteady like a broken reed, with a scarf covering her severely dehydrated and fast disappearing hair. The glow of delight on seeing Maninder lit up her face. Maninder felt a surge of joy whenever she cooked something mild, gentle and aromatic for her neighbour. "I enjoyed your curry," was something she used to hear whenever she spoke with her on the telephone.

However, this situation was not destined to last long. Six months after their first meeting, the big C defeated Margaret and Maninder felt her peace torn apart again.

She did not have much opportunity to help Dr Dharam who

lived two doors away either. Once a successful GP, Dr Dharam was withering away after having suffered the ruthless assault of dementia. Once known as a caring doctor who gave careful, thorough diagnosis for every patient who went to see him, he was now prone to babbling words without context or relevance. He did not leave his house for days and, if he came out of the house for a breath of fresh air, supported by his wife, Shushi, he would walk a few yards in a kind of trance, with glazed eyes, unable to recognise his neighbours. His walking was slightly awkward, unsteady and wayward and his wife had to hold his arm to guide him. A decade before, he'd been a successful GP in Coseley, known for his sense of humour and having a genuine interest in the well-being of his community. He took an active part in celebrations at the local Hindu Temple. On Tuesdays, he would be there at to oversee the preparation of meals regularly donated by him.

Maninder recalled how he daubed everyone's forehead with red dye when it was Holi. He had lost his first wife, but remarried a woman who was ten years younger than him. On one of his visits to India, he was introduced to Shushi who was a widow and they quickly decided to get married in a solemn and very private ceremony. Following his return to England, he sponsored her visit and formalised his marriage in Dudley's registry office.

They felt comfortable with each other and led a simple life in their spacious house. Their only pleasure were going for walks, visiting the local temple and making trips to India every other year.

The peace and satisfaction of giving up work in retirement did not last long though. Starting with frequent episodes of forgetfulness, gradually, over the years, dementia took a tight grip on his life and he completely lost his short-term memory and became truculent, while remaining physically almost unscathed. He did not recognise Maninder or even Shivraj who used to see him often at the temple. He had become a recluse, a seething vessel of churning emotions and half-forgotten memories from the distant past. Maninder did not see him much during the first year of her move, but often noticed an ambulance parked on his drive. Dr Dharam had a son who was in Toronto. He had asked his father to stay with him in Canada, but his indomitable spirit of independence did not let him accept his son's request. He stayed in Stourbridge with his wife, marching towards his final days while completely oblivious to the outside world, lost in the dense fog of half-forgotten memories.

Maninder was not afraid of death and she knew it was a natural phenomenon, the inevitability of which could not be challenged. But the process of dying, the months, weeks and days before ceasing to exist could be the most terrifying experience anyone ever had. She had an irresistible affinity for people who were either suffering or spiralling down towards their final days.

At the outset of spring, whenever she went out of her bungalow, she had Wordsworth's line racing through her mind about daffodils, where he recalled how they were:

Continuous as the stars that shine
And twinkle on the milky way,
They stretched in never-ending line
Along the margin of a bay:
Ten thousand saw I at a glance,
Tossing their heads in sprightly dance.

She liked the space and freedom that her new neighbourhood provided. She could go out of the front door and find herself surrounded by greenery and a profusion of flowers and shrubs. The people living there took pride in keeping their surroundings clean and tidy. In her previous neighbourhood, very few people cared about the environment around their houses. Many of her Indian neighbours had an obsession with possessing Mercedes cars. They used to purchase secondhand Mercs and spend hours and hours washing, polishing, and strutting around them to show off to the world that they had made it. They would do their cooking in their garages or garden sheds, making do with the cheapest ingredients, so long as they had posh cars to declare their wealth. Instead of people in the street gawping at her or twitching their net curtains whenever Shivraj visited, Maninder found the new location a haven of tranquillity.

Her newly-awakened interest in gardening gripped her mind and the look of the plants and grass in her front and back gardens filled her with a desire to learn more about horticulture. She began to find begonias, crab apples, rhododendrons, mahonias, hydrangeas, peonies, camellias and dahlias captivating and, whenever she needed a break, she would traipse to a garden centre or a plant nursery. Her garden had some seasonal flowering plants adorning the borders, such as hyacinths, tulips, antirrhinums, busy lizzies, phloxes and petunias. She found it more interesting to find colourful perennial plants to economise on maintenance time though and so she read up on the vast range of plants available and lapped up all the information she could gather. She began to keep her front garden very tidy and scenic and passers-by would sometimes pause to take in the richness of what she had planted there.

She would target weeds and could now recognise them from metres away. Whenever a new weed was caught rearing its head, she would target it and use a few choice curses to deter future revisits. Shivraj sometimes was convinced that she knew all the weeds by their individual names. Whenever she came back to her bungalow after a walk or a visit, she would first stop to drink in the beauty of her front garden. This used to go on for several minutes, sometimes stretching to twenty minutes or more and, only after that, she would finish her travels around the front drive, unlock the porch door and go straight into the back garden to prolong her pleasure. Drizzly summer rain or a strengthening breeze would not be able to coax her to forego her enjoyment of her garden and make her go inside the bungalow. Tired flower petals, exhausted shrub branches, or the limpidness of any plant tendrils would ring alarm bells and she would not sit still until she had provided support.

Maninder felt contented with life after many times of anxiety and depressive lows. She was able to breathe in fresh air, come and go, invite her friends to her bungalow and have choice and freedom. She loved the secluded setting and would spend hours rearranging the furniture in various rooms to achieve the optimal aesthetic.

Not far from her previous house, there was bustling market for Asian goods, assorted Indian vegetables and fabrics. Every weekend, it used to be crammed full of Asian families looking for fabrics, foods and jewellery. There used to be at least five barbers' shops concentrated in that area of the town to cater for their Asian clients. She used to pass by them every time she went to Merry Hill. But now she went along that route once every two months, if that. Her new lifestyle suited her and she wanted to make the most of it in her remaining years.

The most striking relief about being in her new part of town was the absence of stares. Staring by first-generation Indians was common in her previous neighbourhood. Whenever she walked to town, she used to see even the decrepit old men of her own community gawping at her. And at other women who happened to enter their field of vision. Even old, usually obese, Punjabi women were prone to stare at other women if they could tear themselves away from gossiping or hunting for bargains in the Indian shops.

A very coarse-looking man with a pronounced paunch, wearing a khaki raincoat and with a baseball cap precariously perched on his balding head used to come every day to see one her neighbours in the old part of town where she had spent more than thirty-five years. His friends and his family used to address him as "*bhhaji*", my brother. Maninder used to feel sorry for him as he cut a very sad figure, walking the three miles to her neighbour's house every day. His wife had run off with an African Caribbean man and he was still living in a terraced house close to the town centre surrounded by Eastern Europeans and a thriving community of prostitutes. He used to act as a handy person for his friend who had a couple of houses rented out, carrying out minor repairs. Maninder however, lost all sympathy for him when she saw him staring at all the women walking on the pavement. Probably his eyesight was not helping him as his stares were prolonged and vacuous. In her new location though, people just went on with their own business, exchanging smiles or sometimes saying "Hello."

She could see people taking their morning strolls on the pavement outside her bungalow. Only those originating from Punjab used to turn their necks to have a quick look towards her bungalow. Others would carry on walking taking in the beauty of the greenery and profusion of colours.

Maninder loved the idea of retaining one's independence. Two of her role models were Don and Diane, a couple in her street who were both in their eighties. They lived on their own in a detached cottage a bit further down the road from her bungalow. Don was still driving his car in his late eighties and Diane enjoyed making soups, stews and roasts for their evening meals. Their health experienced many tides of change though as Don passed out once when he was going to the newsagents to get his morning newspaper and the doctors asked him to refrain from driving for three months. Diane, meanwhile, had sporadic spells of dizziness and felt unstable on her feet. Yet they resolved not to go into a care home or to move to their daughter's house in Bridgnorth. Her daughter, Anne, used to visit their cottage every weekend and their grandson, Mark, regularly came to wash their cars and do odd repairs in the cottage.

Don and Diane became very close friends and used to come over to see Maninder every so often to spread a bit of cheer with their humour, news and holiday plans. Diane had a vast knowledge of plants and she used to go through Maninder's garden and give helpful seasonal tips. Maninder was envious of their independence when she saw them happy, walking holding hands, looking after each other and enjoying life without any intrusions from their family members.

She started to spend her mornings going on long walks, traversing the almost untrodden path through fields facing her bungalow. Shivraj usually joined her and the cool breeze caressing their faces brought home the paradise that once she thought she had lost forever. The view of horses roaming in the fields, flocks of sheep following each other, the water gurgling in streams, the soothing sound of leaves rustling on trees bursting with blossom worked together to bring her Eden. She often used to think of the village in Rajasthan where her parents had moved to prior to their move to Punjab. She remembered the vast expanse of fields there with an occasional surprising tree in the desert, the orchards of kinnows and the dance of vegetation in the morning breezes before temperatures soared in the afternoon. It was exactly the same here, she thought, except that it was many times over more orderly and more consistently green with a large presence of tall plants and trees.

She had an emotional connection with a few parts of India, but after having lived here for over fifty years, some of the memories had become the stuff of nightmares, but there were more pleasant parts of her life too, such as going to college in Sidhwan, meeting up with friends in Banga, having a chat with her mother who used to generously dispense ancient aphorisms to encourage her to cope with life after marriage, the time she spent at work with English colleagues from whom she learnt a huge amount about their culture, the protection given to her by Amarjit – Maninder used to spend hours sometimes reflecting on her past.

The biggest gain from moving was the increased time she could now spend with Shivraj without having to think twice. Talking of the days of old with him purged the toxin of past letdowns. After retirement from his job at the probation service, Shivraj had enough time to soothe her pain and replace it with quality time. She became so fiercely independent. She felt she could live life on her own terms without knocking on other people's doors.

21

---

8 September

I feel more and more drawn towards Maninder. She has penetrated the inner layers of my heart. When I first became aware of some feelings stirring within me, it forced me to look at her in an entirely different light – she has a kind of soft radiance of purity found in the fresh snow on the slopes of high mountains, but I thought I was reneging on my love for Puneet. I wondered if I was crossing the Rubicon. But gradually as I got to know Maninder without distance and I became convinced that my emotions were genuine. I often thought of Hilaire Belloc's lines:

It was my shame and now it is in my boast
That I have loved you rather more than most.

To say that Maninder has changed my life would be an

understatement. She has kindled a new love for the beauty and grandeur that surrounds us. Now I look at the swaying blades of grass, dancing flowers in the cool breeze of the morning, floating fluffy clouds across the sky and hear the cadence of the full-throated music of the dawn chorus, all with a fresh, reawakened interest. The world suddenly looks more interesting. Dancing to Mozart or the Noorani Sisters does not feel ridiculous any longer.

12th September

A neighbour in my street never ceases to amuse me. He has been married and divorced twice, each time after a bitter, obstreperous dispute. He has two teenage children from his second marriage. Doing any household work is an irksome activity in his eyes. He makes his son mow the postcard sized front garden and unload the shopping from his car while he is busy taking rapid drags on his cigarette with great concentration and vigour. A few months ago, he persuaded another woman to live with him in his rented house. She is a caricature of femininity with garish lipstick, outdoing teenagers on a night out with friends in her skimpy dresses. He and his new girlfriend must have been treating his daughter like a slave because I don't ever see her outside the house, except when going to or coming back from school. Occasionally, there are noises, harsh and strident, billowing out of the house. One day, the daughter left home under police protection and went back to her biological mother.

2ⁿᵈ October

After Puneet's death, my spells of loneliness have become more frequent and corrosive. Often, I don't need a trigger to slide towards depressive thoughts. The fog of sadness descends without any warning.

I was in a park today, having my constitutional, when I chanced to pass by a huge gathering of fragrant jasmine and saracocoa. The sudden invasion of their perfume made me feel inebriated and then, all of a sudden, I thought of Puneet who used to take her morning walk with me in the same park. Her face swam before my eyes and suddenly I had to wipe my cheeks. I have lost my heaven, the key to my innermost joy.

Maninder has, to a large extent, diluted that sense of loneliness. She has her own obligations to her house, her children and their families and to her relatives though and it is in those long hours of separation that I feel loneliness creeping towards me.

When she is with me, the focus on the moment fills up our minds.

2nd October

Maninder has had a fall on some rain-soaked leaves while out for a walk. Her shoulder blade took a battering and a prolonged, unbearable pain decided to visit her, despite the strong painkillers that she is taking. To make matters worse, she has had a high temperature, her whole body suffering from the after-effects of the nasty fall, causing a splitting headache, so she emits muffled groans and feels completely listless. Convulsive pain courses through her body, but, at the same time, ageing itself is making her feel more helpless than usual. I look at her, a shadow of her former self, a wan face that once radiated grandeur, and I feel sorry for her, recalling Dannie Abse's lines:

All the old gods have become enfeebled,
mere playthings for poets. Few, doze or daft,
frolic on Parnassian clover. True, sometimes
summer light dies in a room – but only
a bearded profile in a cloud floats over.

It took two weeks for her to begin to feel better. She still felt battered, bruised and prone to be shivery though. She who used to make sure that I was properly fed and watered was slightly embarrassed to be recipient of my care.

4*th* November

Maninder is looking at her garden. A few weeds are spreading their tentacles over the grass. She is perturbed and stares at them as if they were alien invaders. She spends much of her time in the spare room, which she has turned into a storage space. It is a place where storage space has been created deployed with great aesthetic sensibility. She changes things and moves storage units around time and time again to find the best fit. She finds it difficult to discard old things. Much of what is stored in that room is the stuff that she once put away years ago just in case she needs it again in the distant future. Scuffed belts, faded trousers, shoe polishes which have not been used for more than twenty years, hundreds of assorted screws and nails and the clapped-out suitcases that she brought over from India after her wedding. It is all there, multiple Pandora's boxes, but she is happy to arrange and rearrange them on shelves, inside storage units, under tables and on the tops of wardrobes. It never ceases to amaze me the amount of care she takes of things which are obviously way past their use-by dates!

4th December

Maninder has been unusually quiet. She is usually talkative, using several sentences instead of one to make sure her point is understood. I am quite used to her prologues and epilogues when she goes over an incident she has witnessed or participated in. But today she had a lost look on her face and words did not seem to be too willing to come out of her mouth.

I realised then that it was Amarjit's death anniversary. She briefly went over one or two salient periods from her married life to go down memory lane. But not for too long. She recited Sukhmani Sahib and then we both offered prayers for his peace in heaven. Is there such a thing as heaven? I find myself asking myself. Has anyone come back to report on that? Or is it only a matter of belief to console the bereaved and those who are left behind? All sorts of thoughts about death besiege my mind.

14th December

I took a trip to Dudley Road in Wolverhampton to buy some ingredients for Indian dishes. The whole place looks very strange, inhabited by people who seem to exult in living parallel lives. There are multiple shops selling similar wares, with what looked like millions of people busy buying lentils, chapatti flour, Indian vegetables, assorted pickles and picking chillies from the trays on display and going for Indian savouries cooked by Haldiram. Nearby, there are two confectionery shops which have a brisk trade. Customers buy dozens of samosas, *pakoras*, fried pieces of battered bread and a wide variety of sweet concoctions.

The glass-covered units contain a line of cooked dishes, both vegetarian and non-vegetarian. The dishes on offer are very unlike the dishes you make at home. The red dyes, the pool of cooking oil at the bottom of the trays and the liberal use of commercially made spices must make these foods attractive only to those who do not cook or who are plainly lazy.

The composition of clients in those shops is baffling at first sight. Many of the customers there look as if they have scampered to the shops after disembarking from a boat. Their clothes, accents and a total lack of awareness of manners when queuing all assault your senses. There are also lots of Eastern

Europeans in those shops, looking for bargains and buying the stuff they yearn for.

There is also a plethora of goldsmiths, buying and selling jewellery. Their shops are like little citadels, with heavily alarmed doors which open only when a button is pressed by the shopkeeper. The jewellery on display is very intricate, gaudy, openly inviting criminals to target those who wear it, which is, usually women.

Very close to this Little India are a couple of *gurdwaras*. Many shoppers go there to briefly pray and then spend some time partaking of the *langar*, free food, below the shrine. Many of them come in their cars, choking the whole car park with their vehicles and even taking over the spaces in the shopping complex.

Maninder and I buy some coriander, aubergines, ginger and chillies and go back to Dudley without lingering.

2nd January

The dawn of the New Year has done little to make my body ache with wishes for the coming months. In the past, I used to look forward to the New Year, with its nostalgia for the year gone and hopes for the next twelve months. Despite age impacting my body, this time of the year used to stir my blood.

But now I don't have any yearnings or dreams for any rainbows to appear across my skies. Life without Puneet has changed my whole outlook on life. I am more rooted in the present. I want to savour life now while I have the opportunity. Maninder has thrown some vibrant colours on the canvas of my mind and that has slowly awakened me from my torpor though.

6ᵗʰ *January*

I bumped into Aileen in the supermarket. She used to be my colleague, working in a different department. But I knew her very well through our regular interdepartmental meetings. Her grasp of the essential priorities for progressing a project was impressive and I used to appreciate her input into discussions.

Aileen had a knack of putting forward her case, interspersed with allusions to everyday life with a joke or two thrown in. She used to take part in promotional competitions. While shopping, she would look out for competitions on wrappers, containers and cartons. She won a good number of prizes because the interest those competitions was usually very low. A box of chocolates, a case of beer, bottles of whiskey, even a trip to New York and assorted shopping vouchers – she used to win a prize almost every week.

But today she looked very weak,fragile and slightly bent under the neck. She greeted me with a big smile, but, in less than a second, that smile vanished. After exchanging inane pleasantries, she told me that she had developed a brain tumour. This news suddenly hit me with such force that I had to ask her to repeat what had just told me.

It all had started when she suffered a few involuntary convulsions and an excruciating headache much of the day. Nausea, lapses in memory and other menacing symptoms appeared later on. She was diagnosed with a brain tumour, which she told me calmly was beyond redemption. The heavy chemotherapy and other medicines were postponing the inevitable, but the end was looming so large, she could almost touch it.

The rest of the day was a goner for me. Life's fragility and vulnerability clogged my mind and I decided to celebrate each new day with thankfulness.

22

Life was a dark, labyrinthine tunnel, a cranny, and I was trying to find my way out, so Shivraj and I were going to a Diwali festival in a park in nearby West Bromwich.

We were talking, not about any particular topic, just making observations on the standard of driving on the dual carriageway. Although both of us were feeling tired and fragile and a bit worn out, we were looking forward to spending an hour or so at the Diwali Mela. This particular mela was a recent phenomenon as it had started some five years ago with a handful of people on a piece of yet unbuilt-on ground alongside Hill Top. Over the years, it gathered momentum and, through publicity and word of mouth, it had become a significant event on the council's calendar. Thousands of people, mainly but not solely Punjabis, gathered there eating *gol gappas*, *pakoras*, samosas and gorging on Indian sweets. There were a variety of rides for children and loud music reverberated throughout the site. Usually, it was

Punjabi Bhangra. As the darkness thickened, there were live performances and a couple of singers from Punjab would belt out their songs for the nonchalant visitors who were content with milling around and spending time at the stalls, browsing what was on offer.

As I released my handbrake, ready to cross a junction, a vehicle from the carriageway on my left crossed the red traffic lights and crashed into me. I saw everything happening, half-conscious of the activity around me. The offending vehicle hit my car on the side, the force of the impact making my car rotate full circle before it came to a stop.

I looked at Shivraj and his eyes were closed and he did not emit a single sound. He was completely silent, entirely unaware of what had happened. I had a sudden panic attack and I began to call out his name. "Shiv, are you all right? Say something please." He came around after five minutes or so when the police arrived and took both of us to the local hospital.

After a long wait in A & E, we were discharged. We took a taxi home, both dazed, in ashen silence. When we arrived home, Shivraj, despite being somewhat emotional, reassured me that both of us were all right, still alive for which we must be grateful to whoever was overseeing our destiny from on high.

The scars resulting from the accident gradually got worse. Pools of blackness appeared on one side of Shivraj's face, but we were happy that we were still alive and relatively well.

Thoughts of death surfaced more frequently in my mind though. As I am getting older, I knew my sojourn on this earth was going to be short. The road ahead is a cul-de-sac. Often, some high and low points thus far replayed before my eyes. The unconditional love of my mother; the yearning to go to university rather than acquiring sewing skills; landing in England where I was a complete stranger; time spent with some work colleagues who had a similar experiences and backgrounds; the purchase of our first house; planting rhubarb stalks in the garden; the debilitating illness that had afflicted Amarjit; my closeness with Shivraj and the accidents that physically sapped my energy – it was akin to watching a film. I am watching myself as if I were another person. And I knew it was all going to end in the near future. I experiences an ache when I feared that something sinister was going to happen.

Nothing gave me more pleasure than going to a place away from my hometown to have a break with Shivraj though. Even when we went to Blackheath, a dystopian hellhole of a town, I felt a breeze of freedom caressing my face.

The taste of what was deemed forbidden by members of my own community has opened doors to new experiences. The Lake District with all its pristine grandeur, Cornwall where peace could be almost touched and savoured, the Peak district with its undulating hills, the beckoning vistas of the Welsh landscape – all our excursions and outings have shown me in abundance the beauty surrounding us. Our short stays in Amsterdam, Budapest and Canada have changed my outlook on life entirely. My perspective on life has become more positive and I readily find awe and wonder coursing through my mind.

It has all made me pause and reflect on what life has to offer if only we can open the windows of our minds.

I find it mesmerising when Shivraj loses himself reading Elizabeth Barrett Browning, John Keats, Emily Dickinson Yeats and above all, Shakespeare. That has inspired me to read the poems of Amrita Pritam, Shiv Kumar Batalvi and Bulleh Shah. He is always encouraging me to read more regularly. After having spent almost fifty years busy with household chores, it's hard to give up those habits though.

I bumped into Dalbir a couple of days ago. I ask her about Ranjit and Kirti. Ranjit has immersed himself in his second marriage. He is still working as a mechanic in a garage and his wife, Samantha, has taken up a job in a care home and their children still attend school irregularly. They like going to Ibiza and Grand Canaria. Ranjit has developed an obsessive fondness for ales and downs several pints every evening. Samantha does the same so that, "he doesn't feel alone." Dalbir has not seen Kirti for several months. Kirti has left her job at the factory. After Jaswinder's fatal accident, she has become a recluse, a huge wall of silence towering around her. And she has stopped ringing Dalbir as she used to before tragedy struck.

I see my children regularly, but every time I spend time with them, I realise that they have their own priorities, their own list of must-do-things to make their life more bearable. They talk about their jobs, their children, their plans for their houses or holidays. Though they ask me about my well-being, I can't see any urgency, anxiety or any desperate desire to listen to my woes or otherwise. They spend a day or two with me and then they return to their own world. This is what has been happening for hundreds of generations, but I do not have any real complaints about their indifference. When I left India and made my home in this country, I didn't give much time to the well-being of my parents who were five thousand miles away. I somehow assumed they would be able to look after themselves.

It is not possible for me to feel settled though as I have feelings of anxiety looming. I know I cannot live with Shivraj under one roof and that is tearing me apart. Rootlessness follows me like my own shadow. Living on my own, very comfortable though it is, has its own shortfalls. My mind often becomes a theatre where events from my distant and recent past strut past, giving rise to memories that I do not always welcome.

I do not see any affirmation of my situation or any sympathy for my loneliness from most of my relatives. Even from members of my extended parental family. If I can't attend a wedding of a distant relative in India, they take umbrage and suggest that I have committed a cardinal sin. They do not pause to think about the bouts of ill health that I sometimes have to contend with. They do not give a moment to consider my desperate efforts to save enough to pay my bills and make my house my home. Their unempathetic attitude when I try to explain my predicament is very hurtful. Sometimes, I even get paranoid.

As I age, and I think I am ageing fast, my mind is frequently overcast with dark clouds concerning the abrupt cessation of life. The other day, Basant, a friend's nephew, returned from work, had a glass of pale ale, ate the curry his wife, Shindi had cooked, went to bed, but failed to wake up in the morning. He had suffered a cardiac arrest and his end came while he was asleep. No pain, no cry for help and no goodbyes to his wife or son. He had enjoyed good health and had no history of serious illness. And he was only fifty-two years old. One minute, he was relaxing in the company of his wife, watching a Pakistani serial on television and, soon after that, his last breath left his body. He was gone without any premonition. I feel sorry for his wife and his young son. But it is going to happen to all of us, sooner or later, and we cannot hide anywhere as death will seek us out.

As you move towards the inexorable end of your life, much of the news you receive has dark undertones. Three of my distant cousin's children have progressed exponentially. They have amassed a huge amount of wealth. The youngest son of the family, Gurdip, was working for a shot blasting company. He had refined his skills for shot blasting and priming materials for a smooth finish. The primer designed for the metal was the treasured secret formula that the owner, Mr Hughes, and his chief chemist had developed. The quality and durability of what they had formulated swelled the number of their clients, including some big manufacturing companies. The products that they had created were known for ensuring the better adhesion of paint, increasing durability and providing additional protection for the material being covered.

The owner of the business also had a secret formula for

mixing metal colours in the right proportions to give coatings on metal parts more durability. The owner, Mr Hughes, fell foul of the law though in his endeavour to avoid paying tax. He was sentenced to five years in prison. Gurdip, my cousin's youngest son, had endeared himself to Mr Hughes with his loyalty, hard work and reliability. Mr Hughes entrusted his business to him while he spent time in prison in the company of murderers, rapists and common criminals. The sudden downturn in his fortune took a heavy toll on him and he had a fatal heart attack. Gurdip took possession of the small company after paying Mr Hughes's widow a few thousand pounds. Since Gurdip had the secret formula for the metal primer and paint, he expanded the business with great vigour and asked his two brothers, Gurbachan and Harpal, to join him. The business took off and expanded seamlessly. They felt the goddess of money had agreed to reside with them.

The sudden influx of money made them inebriated with ego and vanity. Going to Paris for shopping, organising birthday parties in Tuscany, having their dogs pampered at Harrods, hiring cooks and maids from India – they started to walk six inches above the ground of their past. After a decade or so, they began to drift apart though and the more money they accumulated and spent, the more they clung to wealth. Their intense love for money created a huge, yawning gulf between the brothers. Ultimately, they individually decided to go solo and began the process of dividing up their wealth. Violent disagreements raised their heads during these discussions and eventually they went to court. They built huge ramparts around themselves and stopped seeing each other. As their case was being heard in the High Court, Gurbachan, the eldest, collapsed and was rushed to the hospital. He underwent a heart bypass and ended up in intensive care.

When I think of how they started their life when they were young, working hard in factories, but having a strong cohesive family life, I feel saddened. We are all guilty. We know that this life on earth is transitory, that it is not going to last long. Yet we fight, deceive, stab people in the back for the sake of money which, in reality, is no more than a passing shadow.

23

Kirti came back fractured within after her visit to her ancestral village in India. Despite the change in fortune she experienced after she married Tarsem, she had an aching feeling constantly smouldering in the back of her thinking. She realised it was not possible for her to be of any real help to her ageing parents since her brother had succumbed to drug-taking, which is so common in Punjab. From a fizzy personality, her brother had morphed into someone who was a complete alien, with a frozen, uncomprehending look in his sunken eyes, being in an expressionless trance once he had had his fix. She could imagine her parents sinking into despair, utterly desolate, flailing their arms to keep their sanity.

"*Maa*, *Bapu*, I know I should have come to help you, to hold your hand and support you before the onset of your journey towards a living hell. You raised me with so much care and love, but I couldn't repay anything to mitigate your pain. I was completely helpless. With two husbands gone, life was trickling away from me. I had no one to support me. I had some support from Ranjit's parents, but only because they had a sense of guilt and they couldn't wait to get me off their hands when they found Jaswinder. They knew he was a non-documented immigrant, but did they care? I didn't have a future and my present was an unrelieved nightmare, though a little bit of help from Aunty Maninder kept me afloat. Before I could get on my feet though, you passed away. What thoughts were tormenting your minds when you knew you were going to die? When I look at my son, Amul, or my daughter, Simi, I expect them to look after me when fragilities of old age beset my body. But you had two children, and both of them failed you. I am sorry, *Maa*, I am crying for both of you."

Kirti and Tarsem gave up their taxi hire business after a few years. They bought a fifty hectares farm just out past Whitchurch. It was a leap in the dark, but they were prepared to take risks. In the Black Country, they felt they could shield themselves against far-right racist stampedes, but in the countryside, they were on their own. Although Tarsem did not know much about farming in this country, he attended some evening classes at the Rodbaston campus of South Staffordshire College Agricultural College. He also had a lot of support from Malcolm and his brother, Nigel, who owned the adjacent farm. There was plenty of labour from East European countries available for planting and harvesting, sifting the produce for onward transmission to supermarkets. They specialised in growing carrots, parsnips, Brussels sprouts and potatoes. The returns they got were very promising and helped them in their decision to buy about a hundred Jersey cows. The milk from the farm was being shipped to Qatar every day and proved to be a hit with the residents there. Tarsem did not mind getting up in the early hours of the morning to supervise the milking and storing it in vats. The milking procedures were also repeated in the late afternoon, while pasteurisation, homogenisation, separation and further processing was done off-site after the milk was transported for bottling.

The neighbours in their beautiful village were welcoming and ready to help. They knew they could not become part of the in-village community, but their move did not evoke any hostile feelings in their neighbourhood.

Simi went to the local high school and did her A' levels here. She did not have a burning desire to go to university. She stayed at the farm, pursuing her own hobbies of buying and selling antiques. Amul left school after his GCSEs and immersed himself in farming. He took responsibility for the dairy aspect of the business and diversified into making butter and cheese.

Kirti sometimes couldn't help thinking about Ranjit. He was the first male friend she thought she had fallen in love with, despite their arranged marriage. The icy feelings and unspoken indifference that flowed from him lit a bonfire under her whole being. "Why did he not love me? Where did I go wrong? Why did he run after Samantha?" Similar questions still from piercing her soul, though the pain had become a distant memory.

Early mornings were spent overseeing the milking of cows, making sure the vegetables were being correctly sifted, cleaned, put in boxes and despatched to Lidl on time. The wastage of root vegetables which did not conform to the prescribed size or were slightly deformed was something she learnt to cope with after a lot of heartburn. But she was contented with her life with Tarsem, happy how things had turned out after the juddering starts in her married life in a foreign land. Amul looked like a country gentleman when not assisting on the farm, exuded self-confidence when going to meet up with his friends.

The setbacks she had endured in the past had given her a serious, almost dolorous demeanour though. Even when she was happy, she found it difficult to smile broadly. A subtle hint of a smile was the most she could muster.

24

Christmas came and went. The mistletoe looked lonely, deserted. I had absolutely no room in my entire body for even a tiny breeze of excitement. Twenty years had just passed after the first encounter with Shivraj when his few words, "Maninder, I think I have fallen in love with you" had sent seismic tremors through my body. When the cool light of the full moon was bathing my part of the planet was the precisely right moment to hear those melodious words.

Not that I understood the depth of my "yes" at that moment. I just wanted to press Shivraj's head against my chest to soothe him, to slightly reduce the intensity of his grief after Puneet's death. All I could think was how he was sinking deeper and deeper into the quagmire of his grief. I instantly resolved to protect him, to give him my support and care. I had admired him as a person with drive, striving to achieve, despite the odds stacked against him. He had come into British society and some considered him to be an intruder, someone who might not fit in with their mores. When he got a promotion or plaudits at work, there were some colleagues who were, if not seething, felt a sense of resentment. But Shivraj soldiered on and became a regional manager within his department.

Somehow, his life mirrored my own experiences, though on a different scale. When I was young, a zest for life and a better future percolated through every pore of my body. I had dreams, aspirations and intense desires to make my life meaningful. I wanted to get out of the morass of passivity with the help of education. Time and destiny, however, was not on my side and my dreams came to nothing. The oppressive burden of my gender and the absence of active support from my family, albeit triggered by sudden illness of my father, changed the direction of my destiny. In my new home, comfort and security came first and blunted my ardour to see beyond my present. Shivraj was made of sterner stuff and did not allow any downturns to impact on his dream of taking the path less travelled.

What chokes me at times when I remember him as a person was the warmth flowing from his physical presence. His kindness, generosity and sincerity transformed me completely. Love was a stranger to my thinking, but his steadfastness dissolved all my inhibitions. My love for him became a force I could not resist. The silent hostility that my own community, including my own relatives, had shown made me abandon many of the traditions that had followed me from Punjab. He became my world, my universe and an extension of my own existence.

Shivraj had gone to India for a few weeks. Before setting off for the airport, I remember him going into each and every room of his house, standing in the garden and looking at the plants and flowers with wistful eyes. I remember how he found it difficult to say goodbye to me and how I couldn't find the strength to say goodbye to him. It was strange and somewhat eerie. All through the journey to the airport, he was quiet which I found very unnerving. He was lost in his thoughts, in a different world, perhaps. I still cherished his emails which he sent soon after his arrival in Delhi. Full of affection, anxious about my well-being and, of course, full of how he was missing me. He had gone back to his ancestral village on a day trip and talked about the dismaying breaking of the spell of nostalgia. as the village looked completely different from what he had treasured in his mind. The overcrowded bazaars, the dusty roadsides and all completely new faces he encountered in public places – he found the entire landscape unhinging.

Within a few days after his arrival, he began feeling unwell. Very unwell. He had contracted a liver infection. He complained of being nauseous and fatigued, with abdominal pain. In one of his emails, he mentioned how he was feeling completely burnt out. It happened so suddenly. His emails and messages got shorter and shorter and I could do nothing but worry every moment of my waking time. Perhaps it was the tap water that he might have drunk unthinkingly, I thought. He had his cousin and his family looking after him in Patiala. He was taken to Rajndra hospital, but the infection proved to be so virulent that within a couple of weeks, his condition took a serious turn. His children went over to India to be beside him. Everyone hoped he would make a recovery, slow it might be though. Then there was silence for several days, no news, no update and I was seized by an unremitting panic.

He lost his battle, his will to live and died in the hospital, highly sedated. The end came suddenly. The autopsy revealed that he had also developed liver cancer that had somehow gone undetected. Perhaps it was in its preliminary stages. The very next day, his mortal remains were consigned to fire in the local crematorium and I was not even there. I could only get there a few hours after the funeral.

What was he thinking in the last moments of his life? Did he have the energy to think about anything? Or had the strength to think had been removed by morphine?

I don't know how I am going to survive without my Shivraj. He gave me a new lease of life, opened new doors of adventures for me. But now I find that my life has lost its meaning, its purpose. He used to recite poems most days. I remember the lines of a poem that he used to love to read again and again:

I love thee with the breath
Smiles, tears, of all my life; and, if God choose,
I shall but love thee better after death.

25

20th February

I arrived in India a few days ago. The smog and pollution levels in Delhi are so severe, catching your throat and affecting your breathing.

I stayed in Delhi for a couple of days, vowed not to come back to the blighted city again, and headed to Shimla. My sister, Rupinder, decided to come to the hill station with me. In Shimla, the weather, though very wet after some torrential downpours, was much cooler and reminded me of home.

We rented a suite in the Skylark Hotel for a couple of days. The hotel was a bit of a disappointment; it was clean, but very basic. The windows of our suite opened out to the Mall Bazaar and the waves of noise, shouts of hawkers, and the general din created by the inhabitants who seemed to spend much of their time strolling up and down the boulevard, invaded our rooms like wasps.

In the evening, I decided to meet up with some old friends who I had bumped into while sauntering up the pulsating Mall Road. When I was back in our suite, getting ready for dinner with friends at the Fascination restaurant, I found I couldn't recall the names of my friends. I recognised them, their faces looked familiar, but their names completely escaped me. That was very annoying and also upsetting.

We went to Fascination Restaurant for our meal and two of my old friends were already there. After the preliminary pleasantries, my puzzled looks enveloped their faces. What were their names? They went to college with me while I was in India. How could I forget their names? I asked inane questions about their well-being, hoping they would mention each other's names in conversation. Which they did. Of course, they were Bajaj and Michael. We had a good Tandoori meal with pila rice and naans.

While I was waiting for sleep to fill my eyes and body, I was feeling worried that I was losing my grip on memory. To test if that was the case, I tried to remember the names of some Bollywood actors who used to be monumentally popular in my younger days. I could recall their faces, even some the scenes in some of their films that I had watched, but their names I couldn't recall however I tried.

Well, it is part of the ageing process, I consoled myself, and went to sleep. It was disrupted and I was feeling restless as if something was gnawing my mind.

13th April

I have had problems recalling people's names for many years unless I come across them regularly. But now I have discovered that I tend to forget large chunks of episodes and events that have happened to me even recently.

Walking in the countryside with my grandfather, having a tantrum with my mother, hating some of the incompetent teachers in my middle school, sucking at fragrant mangoes during the rainy season, eating my evening meal on the flat roof of our house –every picture of the past, however, has retained its vividness and detail in my mind.

Perhaps things get exacerbated because Maninder has been away for several weeks visiting her distant relatives in Rajasthan. While in the village, she can see goats and sheep being herded into a disciplined line towards the fields where they are left to graze. She told me that, the other day, she saw a drunken man who was talking to himself and a couple of hours later he was lying in the open gutter with some boys throwing small pebbles at him.

10th June

Maninder has not returned after her very long stay in India. In the initial few weeks of her absence, I felt as if I was on my own, unsupported, abandoned. Clouds of memories would fill my moist eyes. But, somehow, I got used to being on my own, albeit feeling perpetually desolate, shunning people's company and choosing to remain indoors. Cooking lost its appeal, the garden was inhabited by wilting plants, books were left unread.

Maninder had recently sold some ancestral land and Teja Singh was demanding a chunk of the money raised. He said he had been looking after the land for decades. I have met Teja Singh once some five years ago. A really coarse specimen of humanity, uncouth, unvarnished, prone to using slang in his thick Punjabi accent that I found difficult to penetrate.

While in this country, he lived in the Berkshire village of Eastbury, working on a farm and driving a taxi in his spare time. He did not mingle with the local community for decades and remained aloof. Fond of building his muscles, he was keen to eat ground nuts, sautéed in ghee in whole milk every morning in a big glass with shreds of dried dates floating on the top. He also spent a lot of time doing exercise in his garage, such as press-ups, planking and other several other contortionist activities. For the last five years, he has been living in a house that he has built in his ancestral village in Punjab. He was enamoured with the idea of having lots of doors in his house. Just as in England, some councils have a penchant for roundabouts. Even if a door was not needed, he would have one installed so that he could boast his house was, indeed, a house of doors.

When Maninder went to visit Amarjit's ancestral village for a couple of days, Teja and his equally boastful wife, Swarni, went to greet her. That greeting turned into a demand for a couple of *lakhs* of Indian rupees. Poor Maninder was perplexed and confused. Teja and Swarni vociferously assaulted her with their claim on the money Maninder had received from the sale of the land. Their claims were drenched in venom. It took a whole week before Maninder managed to contact me for advice. Yes, of course, give the money to the bastards and make your exit from that toxic place, was my advice. It took another fortnight for her to organise a withdrawal of money from her Indian bank account before Teja let her go. She had gone to the village to retrieve some of the things she had been given by her mum at the time of her wedding. She didn't waste any time locating a tuk to the nearest bus station to take her back to Rajasthan. When we learnt about her ordeal, we were very scared and yet relieved at the same time. She took another week to recover, before catching a return flight to Birmingham. Since that episode, she has not mentioned visiting India again!

ABOUT THE AUTHOR

Sehdev Bismal has been living in his adopted home, the United Kingdom for over 42 years and has made a substantial contribution to relations between different ethnic and faith communities in Wolverhampton.

He was a Head of Service in Education for over 20 years and witnessed seminal changes in schools, local authorities and a range of contradictory responses to the increasing presence of people from different backgrounds, ethnicities and faith traditions. He has regularly written on these issues emphasising the need for dialogue, understanding and cohesion between different communities.

OTHER BOOKS
BY THE SAME AUTHOR

Dream Interrupted (2009)

Available in paperback on Amazon.com